Helpless Sins

CHAPTER 1

Mary's eyes flickered open to the first rays of light creeping into her bedroom window through the sits of Venetian blinds. Half asleep she shifted under the covers to the feel of the linen caressing her naked skin and suddenly, as if woken from a dream, a reality that should have only been a dream sank into her mind with unerring accuracy. Slowly as if to prepare herself for some horror or delight, she rolled her head to the side to see the young man still deeply asleep beside her. His adolescent clean skin gave a neat glow in the morning light and his unkempt hair was strewn along the pillow he laid his head on.

"Oh God..." She whispered almost inaudibly before closing her hands over her mouth in an afterthought to not make a sound. Mary lay trying not to move; trying not to breath for fear that any stir might awaken her son Paul and force what she had done into an even more terrifying reality than was already causing her such distress. As she looked him over, her heart and her mind tangled with deeper more primal senses inside her, battling internally as to what had been her greater sin only hours earlier; what she had done, or the fact that even now she couldn't help but need it to happen again. As she struggled with an internal frenzy her mind played the deeds of the last twenty four hours back in full color high definition.

Saturday morning...

Slipping off her pajamas and laying them out across her dresser, Mary customarily stood in front of an antique mirror in the corner of her room and looked herself over. She turned from side to side, checking all available angles. She patted her flat stomach approvingly and smiled to herself. At the middle age of forty and one failed marriage under her belt, Mary prided herself in keeping in shape where so many of her friends had begun to slide. Her divorce had left her with a struggling self esteem that she worked hard to gingerly mend by staying healthy. Her husband had traded her for a younger model; a blow that had made her think a lot about competing with more slender and curvy competition out there. Still in spite of her condition these days, she had discovered the dating game to be one for the young. The occasional man who had been caught by her presence had proven little more that a one night stand upon discovering that Mary was also a mother. Few were willing to accept that extra baggage and she had all but resigned herself to being the target of a 'hit it and quit it' romp.

Nevertheless, as she admired the reflection before her she still was satisfied with what she saw. Mary was a taller woman than most of her friends, measuring in at 5'10. Being mid January, her skin had lost all of its summer glow from tanning but adorned her body tightly, and in tandem with her less than naturally bright red hair and deep sea green eyes, she had the look of the hot Irish women she had heard men discuss fondly, though being a naturally blond woman from the eastern seaboard, nothing could have been further from the truth. Her figure was toned and fit; the product of several years since she had first taken an interest in yoga and jogging at the recommendation of friends and her bottom and sculpted thighs were a tribute to how hard she had worked at both. Mary prided herself greatly on being able to fit comfortably in jeans that didn't bear any labels that said relaxed fit. As years had gone by she had become less and less satisfied with her breasts. They had lost some of their youthful firmness and bounce, but nothing that wasn't fixable with the right bra and excellent posture and where their contour had begun to slack, their size had always caused men to believe that they were less important than her face. It didn't bother her much and her wardrobe was abundant in low cut tank tops to give notice to her cleavage.

Abandoning her ritual morning vanity at last, Mary rounded her bed towards her closet to fetch suitable running attire, winding her long hair into a pony tail as she rifled through her shirts. After sliding her shorts up her legs she was about to make her way from her room when a shiny reflection caught her eye. Out of her window and down the lawn, her son Paul's car shined brightly in the morning sunlight. Mary cocked her head, eyeing the car with curiosity. At 18, her son was a social young man and very active to say the least. It was uncommon, even in winter for her to awaken on a Saturday to anything but an empty house, even as early as it was. Be that as it was, the 2003 Trans Am gleamed pearlescent silver in the sunlight. Thinking little more of it, Mary sat on the edge of her bed, slipped her running shoes on and made her way into the hallway towards the bathroom for morning necessities before she hit the road.

Passing her son's room she took stock of the fact that the door was open but Paul was not to be seen. It wasn't until she approached the bathroom door at the end of the hall nearest the stairs that Mary paused to the subtlest of foreign sounds. The faintest hint of the electric hum given off by the downstairs television hissed in the air. Mary paused again; this was uncommon. Paul wasn't much of a TV fan. In fact he rarely spent any time in front of it. He was more the outdoorsy sort and was always much happier to get out of the house with friends first thing than waste his time on a couch. Mary had always attributed this quality to her son's many successes. Unlike many of the boys his age who would have been happy to spend an entire day with a videogame if left to their own devices, Paul got out, did well in school and had a booming social life. Everyone in the neighborhood commented on him and praised Mary for her successes as a single parent. Venturing into the more bizarre, while she was certain the television was on, she couldn't hear anything coming out of it. Deciding that nothing could really be as strange about the situation as she was building up in her head, Mary tended to her morning needs in the bathroom and started to make her way down the stairs.

"Oh shit..." Came a soft but forceful whisper as Mary looked up from her feet and into the back of the living room only to nearly fall right down the remaining stairs as she stopped dead in her tracks. The large flat screen at the other end of the room was indeed on and the screen was graced by a young man relentlessly taking an older woman from behind with all the intensity he could muster while a younger girl more the man's age lay beneath the other two, happily lapping at the man's testicles with her out stretched tongue. Though despite the fact that the porno no doubt had audio of the women screaming in pleasure, the television itself was muted silent. The only other motion in the room drew Mary's eyes from the screen to the sofa where her son Paul sat, clearly oblivious to her presence as his hand flashed rapidly up and down the shaft of the largest cock Mary could ever remember gazing upon. Other than a pair of open jeans, Paul sat staring at the screen unclothed. His chest and forehead were damp with perspiration. His dark hair was still the tangled mess it had been when he had rolled out of bed that morning and gave him a bit of a wild, bad boy look. His slender lips were apart, quietly breathing hard but Mary barely was able to take notice of these characteristics. Clutched in Paul's hand was a cock that Mary felt instantly certain any woman could have been able to stack two hands, top to bottom along the stalk, and still have more sticking out the top. Moreover, her son was a man with larger hands than most and even as one tugged along the monstrosity erected from his jeans, even he was barely capable of closing his fingers completely around the thickness.

'That's defiantly not his father's genes at work.' Mary mused to herself. His manhood was rigid and shiny; gorged with blood to its threshold and the dark pink head spilled pre-cum down across Paul's fingers to such extend that it nearly looked like he had already orgasmed and simply hadn't stopped jerking off yet.

Mary remained on the sixth step from the bottom taking in the sight. Whether it was because she was herself rather sexually deprived of late or because of the magnitude to her son's best kept secret, she was unable to take her eyes from him. She watched in awe as time seemed to slow in that moment. She stared intently each time her son's hand crested over his cock before flashing back down the shaft again, each time squeezing it so that more of its salty sweetness dribbled over. Mary's vision tunneled until everything but her son's cock went into a hazy blur. Unconsciously, she felt her tongue lick across her lips as the mouth watering sight seized her with all the seeming of some beast that had caught her throat. The more she stared, the more she appraised her son and she wondered a moment if she had taken hold of his cock what its slippery rigidity would feel like in her hands. Not more than a moment later Mary shook her head violently as just a flash of what he would taste like; his pre-cum oozing out across her tongue...

'What the fuck are you thinking?!' She scolded herself. In spite of her better reasoning however her eyes locked right back on Paul's hand as it passed up and down his glistening manhood. Before Mary could decide whether to creep back upstairs or announce herself with some false maternal authority, Paul's face tightened and his teeth clamped together. Just when Mary thought she had regained any semblance of proper parenthood she watched in awe as her son's semen erupted, thick and white from the head of his cock in four harsh streams that splattered against his hand and across his stomach. 'Oh... my God!' Mary admired the spectacle with the commanded attention that would have been better appropriate to watching any other man ejaculate than her own son. 'So much...' As Paul continued to jack his cock through his clearly well developed orgasm, his hand milked more and more semen from the tip. Mary shut her eyes trying to block the image, but her mouth had once again begun to water.

All her life, Mary was the sort of rare woman that most men were pleasantly delighted to encounter. From an early age she had been sexually aware and it wasn't long before she discovered one of her favorite proclivities was oral sex. Specifically, she had always been aroused by the sight of a man's climax but even more to the point, she was almost incapable of ignoring her lust for the flavor of a man's semen. She had tried for years, among friends, to reason her addiction to it. Something about trying to describe what she yearned for in terms of taste and texture had always fallen short however. It was, very flatly, something she loved. Now however, she found herself trying to be small and silent, shutting the beautiful image before her out of her eyes in hopes that when she opened them everything about her surroundings would be normal again.

"Fuck!" Paul's voice sounded in her ears, shattering all delusions that there was any way out of her current predicament. "Mom?!" He called her way with a heavily embarrassed tone. Mary opened her eyes a crack to see him tucking his still swollen cock back into his jeans.

"Sorry!" She replied as she turned her head away all together. "I didn't know you were in here..." She tried to lie as she peeked back again through half closed eyes to see Paul rising off the couch and clicking the TV off. "I didn't really see anything. I'll go back upstairs and you can just..."

"No I'm... I'm leaving anyhow." Paul replied as he tossed a shirt over his head as quickly as he could. Mary watched as the wet spill on his flat muscular stomach seeped through the fabric as it rested against his body.

"Paul you don't have to... I mean it's not like you were doing anything wrong." Mary pleaded trying to be composed and mature about the situation.

"No I'm meeting a friend and... I'll just be back later ok?" Paul shot back with a red flush overwhelming his skin as he dashed from the room with hardly a backward glance. Mary sank to a seat on the stairs as the sound of the front door opening and closing left the house quite silent. Staring at the couch where her son had just been, it was as though a ghost of Paul had been left behind. She watched the imaginary young man, still cranking his fist down over his cock; gasping in manly pleasure as streams of his pearly essence spilled across his chest. Without realizing it, Mary had begun to breathe just a little faster as a familiar tingle somewhere deep inside her began to prepare her neglected womanhood with a thrilling rush of warmth and moisture.

"Oh my fucking God!" She screamed as she sprang to her feet just as her hand had smoothed down over the crotch of her shorts. "What the fuck?!" She shouted again into the empty house as she flailed the same hand in the air before her as though trying to shake off something awful or terrifying. Stepping down the stairs and into the living room, Mary became faintly aware of the faint scent of her son's perspiration. Hastily she rushed to the window, flinging the pane upward to ventilate the house of her son's pheromones. Then as though aware through an out of body observation at the mania she clearly had to be displaying, the urge to break down in laughter caught in her throat. She stopped, closing her eyes, trying to center her thoughts as she patted the sweat from her palms against the fabric of her shorts.

"Alright, get a hold of yourself." She exhaled, shutting her eyes in an effort to bring her spinning world to an immediate halt. "This is simple. It's been a few months and the first cock you see is going to make you horny no matter who it belongs to." She reasoned aloud. 'Never mind the fact that that cock was absolutely beautiful, and something about watching your own son masturbate was the most erotic experience of your life.' Came the inside reasoning of the devil on Mary's shoulder. The simple truth of that struck her blatantly. She couldn't deny it; it was true. It was more than just hormones coursing through her neglected body. The more she replayed the spectacle she had witnessed, the more the truth sank in; it was the sexiest thing she had ever witnessed because it was Paul. This startling discovery derailed Mary's calm to the point where the heat between her slender thighs was becoming frightening.

All of the sudden it hit her; an outside voice of reason was all she needed in this moment of uncharacteristic weakness. Her best friend Samantha had always been her sounding board in moments of need. Mary dashed into the living room and dug her hand into her purse, rummaging around until she found her cell phone. Frantically she passed her finger over the screen until Samantha's name came into view. The line opened, bringing the sound of a ringer into Mary's ear for several moments before going to voice mail.

"You've reached..." Her friend's automated sounding voice chimed through the phone. Mary muttered under her breath as she drew the phone away from her ear to try to call again.

"Come on Sam, pick up!" Mary whispered to herself as she re-highlighted her best friends name on her iphone and hit send again. The ringtone sounded for several seconds more before the line clicked in.

"Hey babe! I almost didn't hear my phone; I was running the vacuum." Samantha chimed merrily.

"I think I'm going insane! I don't know what's going through my mind right now. I'm a mess!" Mary rambled, skipping the opening pleasantries as she paced her living room rapidly back and forth. "I need a reality check."

"Sweetie, slow down." Samantha reassured in a clam voice. "You're talking like a train with no brakes. Just breathe..." She instructed while breathing deeply herself in the mouthpiece of her cell phone. "Now tell me what's wrong."

"Where do I begin?" Mary replied with no less a frazzled tone of voice and then she proceeded to lay out her morning and the subsequent results; how her son's form had sent her into such a state that she was certain she was losing control of herself. Samantha listened dutifully with all the silent diligence of a true friend, allowing Mary to rant and rave and spill what had undoubtedly become the grandest skeleton in her closet.

"Alright." Samantha exhaled after Mary had bared her soul. "Have you taken care of yourself yet?" She asked finally after a thoughtful pause.

"I'm sorry?" Mary exclaimed.

"Char, try to stay with me here. It wasn't a complicated question. Have you masturbated?" She clarified so plainly she may as well have been asking what Mary had done to get a troublesome stain out of her favorite sweater.

"You're not suggesting... not while thinking about, Paul?!" Mary protested, clearly taken aback by Samantha's suggestion.

"Why not?" Samantha replied with a slight glint of a chuckle in her voice. "Are you planning to hold it in all day? Clearly you need to address this. Besides, I don't think there's anything wrong with it."

"He's my son!" Samantha nearly shouted into her phone as she flopped down into her sofa, nearly exhausted by the thoughts running through her mind.

"So what? He's a young attractive boy and clearly he's a blessed boy at that. I mean... well, that is to say you aren't the first mother that this has happened to, believe me hon." Samantha trailed off.

"You mean... you?" Mary began.

"Sure." Samantha exclaimed.

"You mean you and Ben..." Mary tried to begin but the words stuck in her throat, not wanting to actually ask her lifelong friend if she and her son Benjamin had ever crossed such a line. Ben was about Paul's age and one of her son's best friends much as Samantha and Mary had always been.

"No." Samantha replied in what seemed like an almost depressed tone of voice. "I'm sorry to say that I've never been brave enough to ever try. But it's crossed my mind of course. Actually, it's been one of my favorite fantasies for years. I think it's just one of those repressed things in everyone's mind, you know? Something psychological and all that; who knows. Personally I've never bought into the modern concept that incest is such a horrible thing so long as all parties are consensual."

Mary could barely believe her ears. Samantha had been her closest friend since college. She had gone through most of her life believing that there was nothing about her she didn't know. Samantha, to the public eye was a very proper woman. She was well mannered, annoyingly polite, actively involved in the Church that she and Mary attended, a devoted mother and wife; certainly nothing about her would ever have suggested such perversions might linger in her mind. Mary had always considered herself the wilder one between the two of them. Sexually, Samantha had always come across as reserved and private. To hear her condone incest, let alone say the word masturbation was new territory in their friendship.

"Listen..." Samantha continued. "I'm not telling you to jump Paul or anything. But you wanted my 'reality check' and this is it. Take care of yourself before this desire of yours becomes too big to control, and if the day ever comes when you decide to take it a step further, all I can say as your friend is, you'd be my hero and I want details!" She giggled.

"My God, Sam!" Mary piped into her phone.

"You wanted my advice." Samantha replied simply.

"I wanted you to talk sense into me, not toss me deeper into the pool and hold me under!" Mary attempted to reason. "Besides, even if I were to take your advice... its wrong! It's immoral, it's sinful; everything about the idea itself is so fucked up I don't think I could even get off!"

"Oh I doubt that." Samantha cooed playfully. "Trust me, it's the taboo that makes it hot. If it wasn't then you wouldn't be as wet as I'm sure you have been since you saw Paul."

Mary was dumb struck into silence. A million remarks entered her mind to retaliate but the moistening reality between her thighs confounded her into silent acceptance of Samantha's logic. The air on the phone stayed silent for a few seconds before her friend broke in again.

"Look, are you alone?" Sam began.

"Yes..." Mary whispered.

"Good. Then I want you to shut your eyes and imagine Paul above you..." Samantha continued.

"Stop it Sam!" Mary groaned.

"His strong arms on either side of you..." Samantha continued, ignoring her friend's demand. "His eyes piercing into yours as he shifts your thighs apart with his legs until you look down your body and see his magnificent young cock pointing at your cunt."

"I'm going to hang up. Stop being dirty." Mary threatened in vain. Despite what her morals were screaming at her, the walls of right and wrong were crumbling down.

"Look at it Char..." Samantha continued with a moan. "So hard... my God just imagine that thick purple head spilling pre-cum and it's pointed right at your dripping sex."

"God his cock does drip so much of it... GOD! I can't do this! He's my son Sam!" Mary cried out as the hot well in her eyes threatened to overflow in tears.

"Let yourself go Char..." Sam whispered. "Touch yourself and let me help you."

"I can't!" She sobbed as the tears broke free and dripped hotly down her cheeks, yet in spite of herself, Mary had begun to slide her jeans down her hips and over her legs until they crumpled at her feet on the floor below her couch.

"He leans down and brushes his lips against yours. He knows you want him and he loves you. You can see it in his eyes. Look at his hand, Char. He's taken hold of his thick 18 year old cock and he's guiding it forward. Oh baby, you can feel it; the heat of his head pressing your lips apart softly." Samantha teased in little higher than a seductive whisper.

"Oh god..." Mary gasped as her hand sank involuntarily into her panties to her swollen clit. The sensation of the simple touch drove her back to arch as though she had never been touched before. With little hesitation she began to slowly pass the length of her fingertips across her sex.

"You kiss him back. You show him your need and passion for him in the tenderness of your lips and he knows, Mary... he knows its ok. He presses in. Oh baby do you feel him? Can you feel his big fat young cock sliding into you?"

"Yes..." Mary whispered back as her fingers moved down over her clit and forced her opening apart. "Oh yes, Sam I feel Paul inside me. Oh God help me..." She trailed off as her fingers probed in and out of her vagina. "Sam... oh God tell me how horrible this is. Tell me I'm going to Hell..." She groaned as she felt her juices flow harder along her fingers. As though not in control of her own actions anymore, Mary proceeded to fuck herself vigorously with all the skill her hand could manipulate.

"He sinks into you, over and over. Your eyes widening with the depth the head of his cock can penetrate you. Oh sweetie, he's so deep every time he thrusts into you that he pounds your cervix. You can feel his balls slapping against you every time he takes you. You're his now..." Samantha gasped, bringing Mary back into reality only just enough to suspect that Samantha's idle hands were up to no good as well. Something about her best friend touching herself too as she led Mary on this journey only made the experience that much hotter. Her clit burned with overwhelming sensitivity on levels no lover had ever brought her to before. She was lost and she no longer cared. Over the phone, Samantha's breathing had become rapid and raspy.

"Oh baby that's it..." Sam egged. "Let him take you. Let your son have you. Give in to him. Look down your body and watch his cock vanish inside the womb he came from..."

"Oh fuck you..." Mary groaned at her friend. The simplicity of that notion hadn't yet occurred to her; to imagine Paul fucking where she had birthed him from only 18 years ago, bringing her body and their relationship full circle. Her loins began to tremble and she stabbed her fingers in and out faster. "Oh you bitch, I'm going to cum..." Mary panted as she dug her fingers in and hooked them behind her pelvic bone to stimulate the spot that would make her release the hardest. Her thighs trembled as Samantha moaned approvingly in her ear and told her to keep going. All at once the waves of torrid rapture reverberated from Mary's core. Her climax clamped her muscles hard against her finger as she felt her womanly ejaculation seep past them and down into a very tangible puddle between her legs that saturated her sofa's upholstery.

"Jesus... fuck... oh God forgive me..." Mary panted as she coaxed as much stimulation as her cramped fingers could muster into her explosive orgasm. On the other end of the phone, Samantha's own labored breaths softly subsided and a silence fell between the friends a moment as each composed themselves in a heavy afterglow.

"Well!" Sam finally stated flatly. "I need to clean up before my son gets home so I need to leave you to it Char. Do you have a better handle on yourself now?" She asked.

"What did you just make me do?" Mary whispered. As she slowly pulled her fingers from her aching labia and stared down at the floor before her like a child who was being scolded.

"I made you face a truth that would have driven you mad otherwise. If you need this again baby; if you just need to talk about it, well... you know I'm here, and now at least, you know I understand." Samantha reassured her friend.

"You might; I'm not sure I do though. I feel filthy." Mary whispered.

"Give it time. I'll talk to you later babe." Samantha replied and with a soft click, Mary's cell phone chimed that the call had ended. She stared down at the screen until the backlight faded and then looked at her wall clock, taking note that Paul wouldn't likely be home himself any time soon and wondered how it was even going to be possible to control herself now, if she could even look him in the eyes. She stared back down at the smart phones reflective black face. The woman that stared back wasn't the same one who had greeted her in the mirror that morning. Everything was different now.

The remainder of the day fell behind Mary in a blur. Mechanically, she had labored about the house, vacuuming, doing laundry; even dusting which she usually avoided until she knew her house was going to be graced with company. Anything she could fathom to accomplish was something to keep her mind distant from the ache of longing between her legs, which since her surrender to Samantha's whims had not gone away. She avoided Paul's room in her chores and had even passed by the mantle while she dusted and cleaned to avoid making eye contact with so much as a photograph of her teenage son.

As the sun started to go down behind the rows of houses in her neighborhood, Mary glanced at the clock on the stove as she drew out a pot roast that she was certain after that morning she would be eating alone. She and Paul were not prone to argument but on the rare occasion it did happen, he had a habit of making himself scarce until he figured she had gone to sleep. He would then return safely home and quietly retire to his room and upon the dawning of the next day, regard his mother as though nothing had happened. Such was the way their family operated, in a cloud of passive aggressiveness. Having endured years with Paul's father, who was more the sort to need to fight out any problem he encountered, Mary was usually grateful that Paul hadn't inherited the same short fuse and endurance of temper. No doubt when she got up the next morning, Paul would act as though nothing had happened and by then if she didn't have a better handle on her inappropriate lust, then God help her.

Mary picked at her plate more than she ate before scratching the remains of dinner into the waste basket in the kitchen and depositing the remains into plastic ware containers in the fridge for Paul to eat if and when he chose to. Diving into the plush living room easy chair, she thumbed absent mindedly through TV channels, realizing there wasn't anything on worth watching but repeating the scan several times until exhaustion took over her and she got up to make her way up the stairs towards her bedroom. As she neared the top step her iphone chimed in her back pocket. Hastily she clamored for the phone hoping for some word from Paul. Instead she saw a text message waiting for her from Samantha which she begrudgingly tapped open.

The text read across the small screen in Mary's palm. She thumbed a reply in the negative and sent it off but kept the phone in hand expecting more to follow. True to her forecast, the phone chimed yet again as Mary had just kicked off her shoes in her bedroom and was peeling her jeans down over her hips.

Sam had posted. Mary sighed with frustration. It was late and she honestly didn't feel like trying to have an entire conversation via messaging. Instead she highlighted Samantha's message and hit her call icon.

"Hey there." Samantha purred with mockish seduction.

"Hi Sam." Mary replied as she placed the phone on speaker and peeled of her top.

"Oh that's not a happy tone." Samantha remarked. "I guess things are still, complicated?" She asked with a giggle.

"Honestly, I don't know. He hasn't come home and probably won't while I'm still awake and even if he did I have no idea what I'd say to him." Mary replied flatly with a certain defeat in her voice.

"Who says you'd have to say anything?" Samantha asked. "He's had all day to deal and forget about it; nothing says it was anything but a colossal embarrassment to him. You're probably in the clear."

"The clear?!" Mary lashed out. "What is clear about what's been going through my mind all day? What's clear about the fact that panties I just took off are pretty much ruined? What's clear about our last conversation; do you remember? Where you phone sexed me into fingering myself while thinking about Paul? That ring a bell?" Mary ranted.

"Yeah I did." Samantha retaliated. "You needed it. Hell it sounds like you need it again. This isn't about Paul; it's about you and your struggle with all this. Most mothers who catch their son's jacking off would just scold them for doing it somewhere like the living room instead of their own room. You on the other hand, my conflicted best friend, started foaming at the fucking mouth so please... don't get angry with me. I at least get it and didn't judge you."

Mary fell silent. There was no response to that.

"Look, I didn't mean to snap..." Sam began.

"No. No hon you had every right." Mary sighed. "It's just been, a very off day for me and I need to go to bed. Tomorrow can wait for... for tomorrow I guess."

"You'll be alright Char." Samantha comforted. "Call me tomorrow if you want to talk more... just talk... I promise." She added with a devilish hint of humor in her voice. Mary smiled, said goodnight and ended the call. Tossing the phone aside, she hooked her thumbs under the string of her thong and began to peel it down before she stared with disbelief at the stringy mess that went with them from her crotch.

Slowly and uncertainly, Mary placed her fingers between her legs and rolled her eyes back as they passed over her clit and easily between the swollen wet folds of her lips. With her legs still draped over the edge of her bed like she had failed to completely get into it, Mary began to rub her clit furiously. Her fingers flashed in circles around it, coaxing it up and down and harshly from side to side. She passed its swollen warmth between her fingers, softly squeezing it between them. Her free hand grasped at her breasts, crushing them. The more she intensified her labors the hotter her skin began to feel. The memory of her son's cock, a scepter set upon a beautiful young man, shoved its way through the mental roadblocks of Mary's repression and she imagined him staring at her while he flayed his shaft while she in turn stared back as she masturbated so vigorously in his honor.

Releasing her breasts from a torrent of tugged nipples and slapped skin, Mary fumbled over her head into her nightstand until her fingers curled around the sex toy she kept hidden there. The dildo was large, nothing like Paul would feel but it would do. Its silvery blue colored texture plunged into Mary's cunt as she spanked her clit as hard as she could. The toy didn't vibrate; Mary had never owned a vibrator, but it remained her favorite lonely alternative to the real thing. With a practiced hand she pumped it into her depths until she contracted down hard and wailed into her silent house in a harsh and sudden climax. Like a woman possessed she pulled the toy into her harder and harder, fighting to continue fucking herself before the orgasm could even subside. Kicking her legs back up onto the bed with her, she pulled one back into her arm to allow her masturbations more depth. The dildo moved so freely inside her, Mary had to slow her efforts, but only enough to avoid losing hold of it inside her all together. Her juices flowed around the shaft of the substitute as she clamped her eyes shut and allowed herself to imagine Paul cumming. Her hands smeared the pearls of sweat gathering on her heaving chest as she envisioned her son's milky hot gift streaming onto her breasts. Harsher and harsher she hammered the toy into herself.

Her orgasms were coming to her faster and easier than she had ever experienced. Lost in the indescribable pleasure, the world around Mary had faded into blurry shapes and half heard white noise. Such was her concentration on her self-gratification and the lewd wet sounds the toy inside her made each time she drove it into herself that she had been totally unaware of the rumbling throaty moan of Paul's car exhaust, nor had she taken the slightest notice of the front door of her house creaking open and colliding shut with the door frame.

"I guess this makes us even." Came a startling voice that forced Mary to rock her head back forward. Standing in the door of her bedroom was Paul, staring at his mother intently with a glazed look in his eyes as she lay before him, spread across the tangled mess of linen, her body moist and flush and the silvery toy still held firmly in her grasp as she stared back up at him motionless and uncertain.

"I suppose so." Was the only reply Mary could muster. For a moment they just exchanged unblinking stares at each other that seemed to penetrate into something beyond each other's physical form.

"I guess... I should leave you alone." Paul remarked as he slowly averted his eyes with all the seeming of a man who didn't want to and began to turn from the door. A sudden burst of courage overcame Mary, so bold that she was scarcely certain if her words had actually escaped her lips.

"Is that what you want?" She asked, her voice cracking with fear. She had begun to cross a threshold. The next few seconds were going to decide much about her relationship with her son. The mix of excitement and terror spun around in her mind like a rollercoaster. Everything was happening faster than she had ever expected.

"What I want? What is this mom?" Paul turned back, trying to look his mother in the eye but even still his eyes wandered up and down the naked woman lying before him. "I mean first this morning, which I'm willing to chalk up to an accident if that's what you tell me it was." Paul began. "Now this, which based on all the little details; you not closing or locking your door, how you are being so frank right now..." He added then paused long and hard searching for his next thoughts. "This seems more intentional." He finally stated. What was dawning on Mary through his words however was the maturity and composure her son was displaying.

"This morning was an accident." She replied, trying to appear as sincere as possible. Her eyes looked at him with a longing for belief. "But, I liked it." She added, feeling her courage begin to slip away as the truth was finally out in the open. The fixed gaze she had previously held on her son's eyes gave way till she stared down at her bed between her still spread thighs. 'Shit, I've fucked this up!' She thought as she felt Paul still staring at her. The look was even more penetrative now. 'Any second now, he's going to turn around and leave.' She thought. Even her inner monolog sounded terrified in her head. But the feeling of the stare down upon her continued, until it was so fixed and unbearable that Mary raised her head again to face the young man before her. Paul's face was now mildly similar to her own. He looked conflicted. "Paul, please say something to me." Mary whispered, feeling familiar tears about to spill down her cheeks.

"You... liked it." He repeated at last. The statement was far more of an affirmation than a question. Again there was a moment's silence. Mary simply looked back at her handsome son as the first tear left her eye as she nodded to him quietly and began to close her legs. She was achingly certain that nothing good was going to come from the rest of this conversation. "I need to know something. It's kind of been on my mind a lot today." He said as Mary whipped her hand across her cheek in an effort to normalize her shame. "How long were you there?" He asked.

"A little while." Mary choked as she attempted to laugh and make light of her answer. He didn't smile or laugh but rather continued to appraise her expression cautiously. "I came down the stairs and I saw the porno first. At first I was kind of irritated but I hadn't even looked at you yet." She explained as she sat up and wrapped her arms around her bent knees. "And... then I saw you and..." The sentence fell short as she stared off somewhere vastly beyond anything in the room. The imagery came flooding back through her mind of the sight of Paul's hand manipulating his long cock into climax. She was certain her face had turned scarlet.

"And?" Paul answered, clearly unsatisfied with the abrupt halt in her explanation.

"It was incredible." His mother whispered almost so low that her meek reply was inaudible. For what seemed like the millionth time that evening a heavy thick silence separated mother and son. Mary's agony was cresting on the verge of insanity. On one hand she couldn't imagine how she had ever gone from the normality of a day before to present. On the other, she was desperate for some validation from Paul. 'Just say anything! Call me terrible mother; call me a whore!' Her mind screamed.

"I'm your son, Mom." Paul finally answered.

"I know!" Mary erupted back, tears spilling down her face so uncontrollably she didn't think they could ever stop. "Sweetheart I'm so sorry!" She pleaded. She wanted to tell him anything to make it right, to convey to him that it would never happen again. She needed him to know that this wasn't her, and that whatever therapy or prayer it would take to make her normal again she would promise him that effort, but the words caught as her sobs intensified. It wasn't until she felt the heavy presence of someone else's weight shifting her mattress that she opened her wet eyes enough to take in her son again, sitting on the edge of the bed near enough to touch him.

"I needed to hear myself say that before I said this." Paul continued as he reached out and placed his hands on his mother's legs as she continued to hold them tightly against her body. His touch was like an electric charge against her already tingling naked flesh. "If seeing me this morning, was half as incredible for you as coming home to you like this was for me..." His voice trailed off. "Mom that was the hottest thing I have ever seen." He said, bringing Mary spiraling out of sorrow and into a state she couldn't identify. "If you had been any other woman when I first walked in here..." Paul began with a more playful look on his face but despite the crooked up grin that was forming on his face, her son's eyes displayed a deeper sincerity, that nullified the need for him to elaborate, and Mary didn't ask. In truth, she was a little discouraged by the comment, wondering how many other women there had been for her son. They had a close relationship, but Paul was normally guarded about his personal life, and not wishing to be intrusive, so long as he never came home with a pregnant girlfriend, Mary had stayed away from the topic of his sex life. On that night, she wanted to be the only woman in his mind, if this was indeed going to be happening.

She reached out, cupping the side of Paul's face, brushing her fingertips along his 5 o'clock shadow before winding her fingers around to the back of his tangled hair.

"Promise me something?" She whispered.

"What?" He asked with the same childish grin until reading her own face he adopted one more serious.

"You stop me if this doesn't feel right." She begged. Her heart was beating in her chest like it had decades ago for her first kiss as she leaned forward towards her son with her eyes closed. His mouth impacted with a firm tenderness against hers. His lips trembled along her mouth, nearly closed, as though gauging her reaction. It was the kiss of a son to his mother that tap-danced on the edge of becoming more with approval, but there was little more sensuality about it. Using her own mouth, Mary cautiously parted his open and slipped her tongue forward. At that moment everything changed. Her tongue was met by his and the firmness of his lips softened and consumed hers. Breathing heavily in through her nose, Mary tilted to the side as Paul took more of the lead. His hands roamed up her legs, parting them open. She could feel the warm air of the room kiss the heavy moisture between her shaking thighs as she scooted closer to her son and let him take her in his arms. Their lips were now those of new lovers, daring to take things further. Impassioned moans began to pass from mouth to mouth as tongues danced slowly in between.

Paul's fingers stroked through his mother's hair and down the back of her neck. Mary shuddered in pleasure at her son's forbidden touch. At once, Paul took her by the throat and gently tilted her head over, breaking her lips form his much to her audible protest until she felt the heat of his kiss around her earlobe, then down along her neck as he positioned himself tighter between her thighs and lowered her back onto her soft bed. Mary sank back against her pillow, letting herself feel her son's moist mouth washing across the delicate skin along her neck and collar. Her naked flesh absorbed the heat of his body against hers as he ground the bulge in her jeans against her naked vulva, making her senses rejoice the way they might have had she wrapped herself in a blanket after being outside in the winter's harsh night.

"Oh baby...my baby boy."She groaned as each nibble, each kiss and gentle suckle of his mouth against her skin tantalizing her body with a jolt that pulsed into her womb. "Take your pants off Paul." She gasped as he bit into her neck firmly. Her back arched in response as she raked her fingernails into the back of his neck through his hair. "Oh God Paul take them off!" She moaned. "I'm been wondering what you taste like all day!" She added as he washed the sting in her neck away with wet purposeful kisses. "Don't make me wait any longer. I need you in my mouth!"

With all the adorable speed of an adolescent boy, Paul wiggled out of his pants and kicked them from the bed as Mary tugged his sweater up over his pale muscular chest before helping him roll off of her body and onto his back. He stared in adoration at Mary as she collapsed on top of him, crushing her lips down against his. He gripped her tightly in his arms, holding her against him until she broke from his mouth and began to slide rapidly down his body. Keeping her eyes locked onto his, she let her tongue trail hot wet fire down his chest to his rippled abs, closing her eyes and groaning as she felt his massive erection slide at last between her heavy warm breasts. She rocked there a while, feeling him sliding in between them as she kissed his navel and breathed in the musky scent of his spilling pre-cum.

"That feels so incredible!" Paul gasped as Mary pressed her breasts together in her hands around his shaft and fucked him. The scent of him became heavier as the lubrication oozing from the head of his cock eased the passage of the beast throbbing against Mary's pounding heart. She wondered if he had any idea that she had become so wet that when she finally leaned back onto all fours she felt her juices seep down her inner thighs. She stared a moment in desperate lingering at her son's cock before wrapping her slender fingers around the shaft and angling it upwards towards her face. Playfully, she pumped it in her fist a few times, delighting that it was still dribbling everywhere before she couldn't prolong her need anymore and dropped her open hot mouth down over the head.

She held him there, keeping her eyes closed and savoring him the way a chocolate lover took in every nuance of a fine piece of European fudge. She rolled her tongue in circles around the small plump cock fist, scooping away the manly nectar that coated it. 'Too perfect...' She marveled before she dropped lower, opening her jaw until he could slide deeper in. The salty throbbing skin sank into her throat until she had difficulty and she held him there, deep and warm in her face, like he belonged there.

"I can't believe this is happening..." Paul groaned.

Mary at last abandoned the perfect still contentment and began to bob her head, sucking sweetly on the way up her son's length and parting her lips just enough on the way back down to brush his skin and allow her throat to spill hot saliva out along the perfect cock in her mouth. Her hand held the base of her son's manhood tightly as she reached in with the other, cradling Paul's heavy balls in her delicate fingers. She rolled them back and forth, letting the sweet spit from her lips coat her fingers and move along his most delicate flesh. If Paul lived to be a hundred, Mary never wanted him to remember a woman's oral worship better than this time.

"God you're even bigger up close!" Mary gasped as she let his cock slip through her lips with a wet pop. "Baby I can't believe how big your cock is!" She groaned barely able to finish the compliment before she engulfed as much of her son's manhood as she could with her eager mouth. The taste of her son's essence teased her mouth and drugged her as she bobbed her head up and down. Fingers wrapped into her hair, stroking the back of her head as she sucked her son with furious intent. "You taste too fucking good!" She mumbled around his cock.

"God Mom, I don't know how much longer I can last. Shit that feels too good..." He groaned sharply. Mary tightened her fingers around his base, staving off any climax. There would be time for that, but she wasn't ready yet. Instead she slowly and seductively withdrew him from her lips with a wet plop and lay back upon her bed. Paul watched in awe as his mother parted her legs widely before him. Her smooth bare sex was dark pink and flushed. Her labia were swollen and puffy and wide open around her deep channel which was seeping her oils generously. With an almost intimidated expression on her face, Mary hooked a finger of beckoning at her son, asking him to mount her without a word. He crawled upon her until he sat back on his knelt legs and leaned down over Mary; the same look of slight intimidation and blatant nervousness in his eyes that his mother's displayed.

The two stared at each other in what felt like an endless pause, each silently asking permission to continue; each conveying affirmation. Mary reached between their heated bodies until she felt the hot wet throbbing skin of her son's cock. Wrapping her fingers around it delicately, she pulled it towards her smooth mound until the tip of the head pressed against her labia.

"Take me Paul." She whispered softly. Between her fingers, she felt his cock slide forward as it pushed into her wet depths. Mary's eyes tightened closed and a squeaky wince of discomfort escaped her throat. Even as prepared as she would have guessed she'd have been from her earlier endeavors, Paul was far larger than any toy she owned. The obvious pain was not lost on her attentive son.

"Are you alright?" He whispered very sincerely. His mother nodded slowly beneath him until her eyes resumed their normal shape.

"Go slow honey. I've never been with anyone... your size." She explained. Paul said nothing, but slowly began to press inside his mother deeper, not challenging any resistance her body offered, but waiting for her tight depths to relax around him. When he had entered her only half way he withdrew to the tip before sinking back in. It was easier this time. Mary's expression quickly faded from mild fear to its previous enthrallment. Slowly but surely she felt him pass more fluidly and certainly deeper inside her each time. Closing her eyes, she concentrated on the slow and deliberate sensations inside her. With each penetrating thrust, the pleasure mounted, causing her juices to pour from her like a broken dam.

"Oh my God... Oh my God!" Mary whimpered as her inner walls expanded to accommodate the delicious intrusion. "So much..." She gasped as Paul pressed into her deeper. Her hands shot out, grasping her son's firm ass and pulling him into her. He was gentle, but Mary had never fathomed taking on a man so large. When she finally felt the head of his enormous cock touch bottom inside her it forced her eyes open to meet his. Paul stared down at her, watching and moving according to her reactions. Something about this attention on his part made her heart swell with love for her son; her lover.

"Paul, tell me this is happening. Tell me baby! Please tell me you're cock is buried inside me lover!" She pleaded; wanting more than anything to make these first moments last forever. "Say it!" She gasped as Paul pulled all but the fat head of his cock out and slowly sank it all back into his wanton mother.

"Do you feel that?" Paul panted as he began to thrust faster. "Do you?" He teased until his mother nodded through labored breaths. "Oh Mom..." He groaned in pleasure as Mary tightened her muscles around him. "Feel my cock? Sliding in an out of your pussy?" He grunted as he thrust his hips forward with a purpose. "Look down your gorgeous body." He instructed. Mary fluttered her eyes open and stared down her belly over her love trimmed mound. "Look at your own son's cock sinking in and out of you. Look at us making love Mom." Paul panted. Mary stared in wonder at the torrid vision of her own flesh and blood pounding into her sex. Each time he withdrew, her sticky juices dripped back down towards her opening. It was the most beautiful sight Mary had ever seen. Paul wrapped her legs up around his legs, pressing them back until Mary's knees mashed against her swaying breasts. The new and sudden depth dropped her jaw open into a soundless scream.

"Paul! Paul!" She gasped once she found her voice again. "Yes! Fuck me! Oh Paul, fuck me just like that! So much cock... Oh Paul you have got such an amazing cock! Fuck me now sweetheart! Fuck your mother's insatiable cunt!" Mary screamed. Never before could Mary remember speaking to a man like that during love making. She was usually uncharacteristically timid in bed, at least vocally. Men had often accused her of that much. Now however, engaged in the most primal wrong doing a mother and son could commit, such things seemed ridiculous. It was easy to let go. "That's it love! Make me yours!" She cried out as Paul gave each thrust his weight, driving his cock into his mother with surprising strength.

"I can't believe how good this feels." Paul gasped as he sank as completely into his mother as he could thrust and then held himself still inside her. Mary's eyes glazed as she stared up at her son, while playfully wiggling her hips, trying to encourage more movement. Paul pushed his weight into her harder, driving ever so slightly forward. Mary bit her lip seductively, savoring the feeling of having her depths so blissfully full. Never before could she recall such a sublime contentment. Rolling forward and propping herself up on her elbows, she brushed her mouth against Paul's in soft kisses as she spoke.

"This has tortured me all day baby." She whispered between playful darts of Paul's tongue in her mouth. "I thought you would hate me." She added before Paul's mouth closed completely over hers and his hips began to pound his magnificent cock in and out again. This feel of his lips conveyed his answer without words. It was cautious yet open. It was acceptance. In that moment of feeling her son take her so passionately, she knew he understood. She knew it would be ok.

"Take me..." Mary panted as he fucked her harder. "Paul, take me however you want me! You know I need you... Fuck me all night long!" She begged before covering her mouth to muffle her shrill screams as her son slammed his cock into her so hard that she watched beads of sweat drip from his brow to her breasts. His hands took hold of hers, tearing them away from her mouth and pinning her arms at the wrists above her head along the bed.

"I want to hear you..." Paul groaned as he picked up the pace. His cock slammed into his mother so hard that each thrust made a harsh slap of moist flesh as their bodies connected. "Let me hear you Mom!"

Mary's lips erupted in a steam of wails and lustful screams and half intelligible speech.

She loved the feeling of control he was exerting over her; eighteen years of authority abolished as she became his lover. She had no power, no will. She was no longer his mother; she was simply his. His to pleasure and his to take from. Without lead up or warning, she felt her womb tremble in heavy spasms. The orgasm sent her passionate rambling into a steady scream as she bucked her hips beneath him to meet his thrusts. Each time he slammed into her it seemed to make the orgasm breed inside her depths. She felt feverish; helpless beneath him as he forced her to climax again despite the exhaustion of doing so. Leaning down, Paul closed his mouth over her breast, suckling her nipple into her his clenched teeth. Mary helplessly was taken back to the days she had nursed him and now wished more than anything that she could lactate. Instead she arched her back for her son, letting him greedily suckle his mother's breasts as he invaded the womb that bore him into the world. The ironic completing of coming full circle was divine.

"Oh god...." Paul moaned sharply. The heavy swell inside Mary forecasted what was inevitably coming. "Mom I'm close..." He winced as he fucked her harder and harder. "I can't hold back; you feel too good!" He added, his face tightening as he tried with all his might to last longer for her. Without thinking clearly, Mary dug her fingers into her son's ass and pulling him into her tightly.

"Oh Paul yes...let it go. Cum for me lover! Fill your terrible mother up with your cum!" She pleaded. It was a horrible risk. Having been involuntarily celibate for quite a while, Mary had felt no recent need for birth control. Her night stand contained condoms, but she had never considered using one with Paul. Not that it wouldn't have been a good precaution, but in the evening's intensity, it had been all too foolishly overlooked. Still, even with all that in mind, she couldn't fathom experiencing her son's first orgasm with her anywhere else than inside her pussy. "Let me feel it! Cum inside me Paul! God help me I need it!" She screamed as she felt her own climax building. Not sure if her son would last much longer, she wrestled a hand free from her son's grasp and drove it between their bodies. Like someone deranged, she harshly began to put her clit as Paul's face tightened. Mary closed her eyes and waited. Even the sound of his exasperated moans of pleasure faded away in a perfect moment, as Mary felt her inner walls expand and shudder as Paul's cock twitched over and over, emptying his orgasm into the core of her sex. Harder and harder she stimulated herself as she felt his thrusts begin to wane, until finally her legs trembled with her own release. "Oh my perfect son..." She groaned deeply as she rode the waves of climax. "Oh my baby I felt that so.... So deep... oh my God!" She shuddered as Paul slowly withdrew himself from her slippery gash.

Mary watched as Paul's glistening cock came fully back into view, coated with his semen and her wet slick oils. Eagerly, she rolled over, pulling it to her lips and plunging him into her mouth, sucking him gently. Paul groaned in relaxed satisfaction as his mother devoted herself to his pleasure. Scooping her hair up into his hands like a makeshift ponytail, he watched as she disappeared his shaft into her face, her eyes closed and peaceful.

"We taste so good." She whispered before taking him back in to savor what remained of the taste of their forbidden sex. All of the sudden she felt his hands on her, pulling her in an awkward fashion until she realized he wanted her over him. Mary pivoted; keeping her mouth locked on her prize as she draped a leg over either side of her son's face and lowered herself to his mouth. His tongue dug into her almost immediately, surprising her into nearly biting the tender flesh in her mouth. She relaxed completely, lying upon her son's body as she gingerly suckled and he softly excavated her dripping womb with his mouth. Their bodies were wet and hot, sliding along each other as they devoured the other. Paul's hands caressed up and down her back, finally resting upon and gently spreading her cheeks to permit his mouth better advantage. His lips closed over her clit, driving her to wildly swallow his engorged member as frantically as possible. Self-consciously, Mary held her muscles tight, trying not to let the precious gift of her son's semen leak out into his mouth, but the more he cleverly teased her button with his mouth, the harder she spasmed until she felt herself drain in spite of her best efforts. Whether Paul didn't mind, or didn't care, he continued pleasuring her as though nothing could be more natural. The careless delight of his intensity only made him hotter to his mother.

They taunted and teased each other's needs with devilish tongues and sinful lips until the bedroom windows were caked in a thick layer of steam against the cold night air outside. The bed covers were attached to the mattress by little more than a corner. The rest had been kicked to the floor. Mary felt more alive than she had in years, like a teenager in the back seat of a car for the first time. Her fiery red hair was a disaster and her eyes betrayed the glaze of a woman truly spent and happy. She had cried out her son's name caring not who might have heard her, regardless of the fact that they were in no immediate risk of discovery. Sensibility had been abandoned and given way to the taboo. At last she lay spent and contented, curled on her side against the young man she had raised like some twisted but perfect dream. Wrapped in Paul's arms which still glistened with perspiration, her heart still beat as fast as it had when he first touched her that night, and she drifted off to sleep as the digital alarm clock on her night stand flashed 4:32am, with the feel of Paul's lips softly against her neck and the warmth of his breath in her ear.

Finally, with a mixture of helplessness and longing, Mary leaned in to press her pouty lips against her son's, to await his return kiss, to bid him good morning not only as a mother, but as a lover and to decide with him what would happen next.

CHAPTER 2

"Lord, give me strength." Mary whispered. The tiny rasp of her voice was the only sound penetrating the silence of her bedroom, save the shallow breaths of sleep coming from beside her. Mary had awoken to face the terrible and sensational truth that her son Paul was in her bed, naked as she was and the scent of their passionate sex still lingered in the air as though they had only finished crossing that line only moments ago. Mary's words felt like a prayer in her heart, though she was really only whispering to herself out of a need to talk to anyone who would listen. As the gorgeous young man beside her dreamed into the morning hours, she hadn't the heart to wake him yet to subject him to rambles of incoherent thought on her part about what had happened. As she stared at Paul so attentively that she occasionally forgot to blink until her eyes stung, Mary rolled her thoughts around inside her head.

"Alright. It happened. It's not like you can convince him it didn't." She began over thinking with all the intensity that a complex calculus question might require. "And it was wonderful... perfect... No! Stop that! He's your son for Christ sake!" Mary stabbed herself with her own logic. "This can't continue." She decided flatly, resolved that she would allow him to sleep and when he awoke they would talk. She would tell him how wonderful it was, how incredible he was as a lover. That she loved him and was terribly sorry for putting him in the position they were in but that was the end of it.

"But I'm not sorry." She whispered aloud once more, realizing what she said with the full force of an epiphany. She wasn't sorry enough, was more to the point. As she recalled the delicious feeling of being entwined with his body and the taste of his lips against hers, Mary felt achingly certain that all the guilt and pain that would come from doing it again was an acceptable price. "Oh my God this whole thing is totally fucked!" The thought sounded like a scream in her head. She was torturing herself beyond any decision she had poorly made in the past. Perhaps, she realized, some lines weren't crossed, but not for the reasons she'd always understood. "Alright, one thing is still certain. I have to talk to him. He's a part of this and I need to hear his thoughts on it too." She decided and to her amazement, all the other voices battling to be heard in her mind ceased, apparently satiated that that was the best course of action... for now.

Mary jumped as her son's body unexpectedly moved over and nuzzled against hers. Her instinct to recoil was defeated by the fact that she had nowhere to go. She was already nearly against the side of the bed. His strong young thigh had draped over her hip, pressing his cock against it which with all the stereotype of a young man, had swollen to its rigid potential in the fading hours of his dreams. The heat of it warmed her naked skin, sending her body into an electric state. As Mary lay perfectly still marveling at the sensation, she closed her eyes, feeling her son's steady pulse in the soft twitch of his manhood against her. Any resolve to await Paul's alertness to discuss the previous night vanished as she slid her hand slowly down her body until her fingertips met with the solid fleshy head of his engorged phallus.

Paul's lips parted as he continued to sleep peacefully while she inched back from him just enough to permit her fingers to wrap around him. The gentle thump of his heartbeat swelled in her grasp like it was giving her permission to continue. Despite the eagerness of her intent, Mary couldn't help but be aware that her grip was feeble and shaky as she slid her fingers tightly up along Paul's shaft. Her maternal shame contended with her desire heavily, until at last her hands steadied. Without her eyes to see her labors under the covers, he felt even longer than she had recalled as her hand glided softly from his base to tip with controlled even movements.

"God what's wrong with me?" Mary whispered as she stared up at the ceiling expecting in part that a divine reply should come from above to caution her against this further decent into depravity. Without warning a hot flow coated along her hand and dribbled out along her hip. Mary immediately lifted the comforter to see the intoxicating sight of her son's clear sticky pre-cum evacuating his penis in a heavy flow as she fondled him.

"Stop this! Stop while you can!" Her better reasoning screamed inside her mind, but Mary had become helpless at the sight of her son's hot natural lubricant going to waste under her skillful efforts. Feeling like she could weep at her helplessness, Mary looked back up at her son's sleeping face. His mouth had opened further, panting softly as she stroked her hand along his cock. She wondered if she could possibly be lucky enough that he was dreaming of her. Locking her eyes on his, ready to abandon what she was doing at the first sight of Paul rousing, Mary inched her body downward until she was engulfed in the covers. Soon it wouldn't matter if he woke up, but until then something about him simply opening his eyes to it happening felt safer to her. It was a cowardice she could live with.

"I'm going to Hell..." She panted as she leveled her face with her son's outstretched cock. The head was glistening with his pre-ejaculate and his skin still wore the aroma of her own vagina from the night before. Closing her eyes, Mary held him firmly in her hand, extending her tongue from her pouty lips until it met his tightly stretched skin. The salty mix of their torrid sex enthralled her taste buds immediately, forcing her to lick upward in a single heavy pass of her tongue until her lips crested over the oozing head of Paul's cock. She locked her lips over it tightly, suckling her son firmly for more of the delicious nectar that she now craved like a drug addict. The musky scent of his crotch filled her nostrils like a poppy field, and like a perverted Dorothy of Oz, she breathed him in deeply as she savored the pleasure of his manhood pressing against the inside of her cheek like a child with a sweet. She opened her mouth around him, pressing forward as she swallowed his cock in more deeply, then slowly she withdrew, allowing her lips to pass her saliva in a heavy coat against his flesh to make the next time easier.

"God Paul, why do you taste so good?" She wondered as she gulped with increasing eagerness along her son's forbidden fruit. Each time her lips pinched nearly closed at the tip of his penis, Paul unknowingly streamed more of his adolescent sweetness into his mother's hungry mouth. She continued fellating him, letting it pool in her mouth richly before she swallowed in satisfaction but the yearning in the rest of her body was beginning to cry out for fulfillment.

"Wake up baby." She thought, willing him to feel her need as he slept. Mary grasped him tighter in her hand, tugging at his throbbing hardness as she sucked Paul more vigorously, allowing deep throaty moans to pass her lips and stimulate his tender flesh. "Wake up. God, please just wake up and..." She begged in silent madness. Like the answer to the silent prayers of a blossoming nymphomaniac, young strong hands wound into her hair along the back of her head with a sudden trembling firmness.

"Please don't stop!" Paul's voice groaned deeply with urgent need from outside the protective concealment of the blanket surrounding Mary's aching body. His hips thrust forward gently, sending the head of his cock back in to his mother's mouth. She took it deeply between her soft wet lips and flattened her tongue to caress it as it sank to the back of her throat. She surrendered, allowing Paul to control her; holding the back of her head gently but with no obvious intention of letting her move as he guided himself in and out of her mouth in long deliberate movements. Mary's hand again sought out the flowing moisture between her legs, furiously massaging her clit as her son used her mouth for his pleasure. The act of giving in to him like this, of allowing such abandonment of control was unlike any arousal she had ever experienced. He was making her his, and in spite of any effort she could have ever imagined mounting, she was helpless to deny that she wanted him to.

Mary reached out along her son's swollen cock, raking her fingernails along its length as it pushed forward into her lips until her fingers felt the delicate thin flesh of her son's testicles. They rested in her circled fingers like monstrous olives, his fragile scrotum contorting and tightening under her touch with delicious reactions. Softly, Mary teased them with her tickling touch, cupping them and rolling them between her fingers as her sons gentle thrusts into the recesses of her mouth intensified in speed and force.

"Oh Mom..." Paul groaned. Mary's other hand had become a flurry of motion over her vagina. Hot thick fluid spilled through her rapidly circling fingers as her puckering sex opened to receive them with longing. Paul's cock swelled and receded with each thrust he made into her wet velvety mouth, seeping stream after stream of his manly nectar along her taste buds. Mary moaned a muffled and desperate cry of passion along against his cock as she plunged her fingertips into her core; three at once with remarkable ease. "God

Mom!" Paul cried out again. The more he said 'mom', she more deeply lost Mary sank into the desperate enthrallment that incest now offered. Her own ambition replaced the need for the hold of his guiding hands against her head. She worked her face forward of her own accord as she rolled him onto his back and took a place on all fours beneath the blanket and bobbed her mouth up and down along his slippery cock.

Paul ripped the blanket back, revealing his mother to his eyes. "God that's so hot!" He gasped as he took in the sight of her, on her hands and knees, taking him into her throat with each sinking motion oh her head. She kept one arm draped back along her body and Mary felt certain that Paul could hear the lewd sloppy sounds her fingers were making as she feverishly masturbated. Somehow, that only made her hotter for him.

"Look at me..." Paul begged. Mary looked up from the sight of his cock vanishing in her face into Paul's intense gaze. His eyes penetrated her to the core as though his fixed gaze could fuck her all by itself. The connection forced helpless moans from Mary as she grunted to continue to fuck her son with her mouth. Willing her throat to become an equal to the saturation between her legs, she decided in a moment to allow what she had never permitted of another man out of nervous hesitancy. Gaping her jaw open as far as she could tolerate, she flattened her tongue to keep it out of the way and pressed her head slowly down further. Her eyes shut tightly on their own as Mary breathed deeply through her nose, willing herself to relax as she felt the mushroom head of her son's cock ease into her throat. The intrusion, new and frightening forced her to cough against him, but still she allowed him in further despite the discomfort of a certain gag reflex. Her eyes began to water as the feeling of suffocation swept terror through her nerves but putting aside every warning her instinct to raise back up could muster, Mary sank lower until more of him was lodged tightly in her throat than not.

"I'm actually deep throating! I'm deep throating my own son." She realized as she continued to force herself to breath normally through her nose. He felt gigantic inside her neck. Despite a certainty of an impending sore throat, the desperate look of pleasure in Paul's eyes urged her to continue taking him in, sending endless inched of phallic delicacy into her mouth. Familiar terrors of pleasure and broken boundaries consumed Mary as she drooled against the meaty shaft each time it withdrew. It was becoming easier to take him in, like a virginal pain that had given way to the delights of amazing new pleasure. With new found boldness, she eased her head forward with each deep thrust into her face as her fingers redoubled their efforts inside the swollen folds of her parted labia.

Paul held perfectly still, watching her intently. In his eyes offered a sudden gentle reassurance that she should continue, but only at her willingness. Mary felt the warmth of security and began to try to press down more deliberately with her slowly bobbing head.

He was so deep it was impossible to believe that his heavy looking testicles were nearly resting on her chin. As she looked down the length of his cock she silently wished there was a way to consume them as well if only to bring his pleasure to heights no woman would ever again be capable of. The idea that she could be something to him in the privacy of her bedroom that he would never be able to replace elsewhere made her feel powerful and alive. In that moment of perfect fantasy, Mary came heavily, tugging her hand from her sex to support her against the bed as she screamed in delight against the intrusion she had forced into her throat so deeply. Her pelvic muscles convulsed, sending a squirt of her juices out of her core and down the inside of her thighs with a wet spitting sound. She felt exposed and embarrassed as she tried to look up at Paul who had cocked his head to the side, glaring at the trickle of his mother's ejaculate that at this point was running nearly to her knees.

"Jesus Christ that's beautiful." He whispered as he looked at her warm tingling leg like it was something to eat. Mary's embarrassment evaporated. Had she only the will to take him from her mouth she longed to kiss him, to thank him for how sexy she felt. Suddenly Paul winced. His hands reached out, clutching the sides of the bed like he was bracing himself. It was not a look of discomfort. Mary had already come to know that face well and pulled her head back, gurgling until her son's plump cock head rested between her lips. Eagerly she circled the tip with a dancing tongue as she took hold of Paul's length and began to stroke her slippery salvia along it like some treasured lubricant.

"Mom!" Was all he managed before his penis noticeably jerked before Mary's eyes. Almost immediately she was rewarded by a heavy warm rush, spilling into her mouth faster than she could swallow it. With heavy gulps she drank from her son's cock as his hips bucked involuntarily and his labored breaths broke into manly howls of pleasure. Mary was transported back to the innocence of infancy; the need to suckle and nurse, and it occupied her mind as grossly appropriate that her own child now nourished her craving the way she had once nourished his from her breast. She sucked harder, desperate for the bittersweet blessing flowing over her tongue not to end until reluctantly she finally pulled away gasping for air, having ensured that her son's last drops were not lost to the hot flannel bed sheets beneath them.

Staring up at Paul as she traced a finger up from her chin to deliver a dribble of ejaculate that had escaped her mouth, he gazed back down at her, breathless and mesmerized. Between his legs sat a proud wet cock that had lost none of its rigidity; the blessings of youth. Mary swallowed deeply as she realized that whoever her son was looking at, it wasn't his mother anymore. His pupils sparkled as though his eyes were made of a glistening liquid flame.

"Oh yes. Please let this happen again. No! It can't yet. We haven't talked." She thought as the weight of terror and wonder fermented in her mind to prepare her for what was to come. Paul sat up, reaching out for her arm. His grasp was firm and unyielding. Mary felt helpless as he pulled her forward and directed her to lay flat along her bed as he rounded her body. She watched him silently, battling with fight or flight instincts as he placed his knee between her thighs and scooted them apart only just slightly. Every fiber of her being seemed to beat in her heart with millions of shouting voices, all competing to convey the emotional flood that was welling inside her.

"Yes..." She hissed. "Paul I want you so badly." She whimpered. The words represented the dominate voice in her scramble of confused thoughts. Suddenly she knew that any protest on her part and it would end. She felt secure and safe with herself and above all her son. She knew what had to happen. She knew what she couldn't go another minute without. Mary turned her head away from Paul, rested her head against a pillow and waited to be ravaged.

She groaned in anticipation as she felt the heat of her son's strong thighs mount her from behind. The hot sticky length of his cock rested blissfully along the crack of her bottom as his hands massaged up her back and teased back down her spine with delicate brushes of his fingertips. She lay there, still breathless with the taste of his semen on her tongue, ready to open herself to him. She felt him take hold of himself, rocking his hips back to align his beautiful cock with his mother's wet depths.

"Paul..." Mary whispered as she finally turned her head from the pillow it rested on and looked back over her shoulder at her secret lover. He leaned down along her back to listen, his heat enveloping her and his breath against her ear. "Make me yours." She groaned with a deep huff of air as she felt the meaty head of his cock penetrate her. His lips closed along the back of her neck and Mary's eyes fluttered up into their lids as she scarcely remained aware of her voice crying out while her son thrusted forward, sending his complete girth into her without the slightest resistance. Her body echoed what her heart desired most. She was terribly wet for him, ready to surrender to any manner of power he would send through his cock into her delicate aching vagina.

"You're so hot." He gasped. Mary rolled her head forward, digging her teeth into her pillow as her son began to thrust in and out. His hands stroked up along her arms until they found her hands, clenching his fingers tightly in hers as his hips collided against her bottom forcefully until the sound of their mutual moans of pleasure was augmented with the delightful noise of impacting flesh. "I can't believe we're really doing this again!" He panted as his breath became ragged.

"Then don't ruin it by talking about it."Mary wanted to reply but kept the thought to herself. She didn't want him to ever stop, but was terrified that if he made it feel any more real her resolve would crumble and she would flee her room in agony; to cover herself and face her son as a mother and tell him that what they had done, what they were doing was impossibly wrong. "How can you call yourself a mother?" She asked herself, hoping almost that some part of her would answer. She wondered if the gorgeous young man behind her, driving the perfection that was his young penis into her so forcefully had even the same cares over their situation; she hoped not. In this moment of bliss, Mary dared to wish that Paul felt totally at ease as he took her with such recklessness. More than anything, she wanted to receive him with the same careless joy, as though they were simply well acquainted friends who after many years had discovered each other in a new light.

"Paul!" She cried out in reply. "Your cock feels so perfect inside me! Take me! Take your mother!" She added, hoping that the filthy words would urge him to pound the doubt right out of her. His pace intensified. Continuously, Mary rocked forward along her mattress, gasping in pleasure as her vaginal walls clamped down on the welcome invader that speared into her slippery womanhood deeper than she could ever remember having had before. His hands clenched hers tightly. His body, now slick with perspiration slid along her back with each lunge of his hips. His mouth washed over her shoulder, biting her flesh as he growled through his lust.

"Oh my God baby!" She cried out when her breath found pause for words. "That's it baby, fuck me! Fuck me!" She shouted again and again. Impossibly, her young lover accommodated her with harder thrusts from behind each time she made the demand of him. Mary screamed again, sinking her teeth back into the soft pillow beneath her face. She had begun to surprise even herself. With other men, Mary had always thought it important to be a vocal lover, knowing well how any man needed affirmation, but it was always little more than that. Never before had she ever felt compelled to cry out to any lover with such insistence and had always resigned such lustful ramblings as the stuff of dirty novels. She felt filthier, and that only made her skin flush hotter than ever. Paul released her hands, which she promptly dug into the linen around her until the hammering stab of his cock sent her limbs flying in all directions. His strong grip clasped her waist above her hips to keep her in place as he sat up and rocked his thighs to drive himself against her toned ass better. The new angle drove him against her cervix with hard beating thumps.

"Fuck yes!" Mary exclaimed shrieked. "Harder!" She grunted, allowing the new found boldness in her to run wild. Paul rolled his body into each penetration, giving it the force of his weight. His helpless mother lay beneath him crying out in an ecstasy she was certain she never would have found without her son. She was no longer being made love to; she was being screwed. Her son's movements were pressing her body forward along her bed which creaked and complained under the unfamiliar stress of two lovers with no seeming end to their need for each other. She hadn't been fucked like this since before Paul had been born. She loved him for it.

"Slap my ass Paul!" Demanded the thing that a mother had become using Mary's voice. In reply, a loud crack of palm meeting skin filled her ears as the harsh pain in her bottom exploded into pleasure through her body. She cried out and begged for more. Paul's hand collided again with her ass once more in the same place and again in a new spot until her rear was evenly warm and terribly sensitive. "Oh God Paul again! Ride me! Spank me! Use me!" She shouted as she felt her inner muscles quake with approaching climax. "Keep going! Keep going! Oh Paul, I'm going to cum!" She pleaded. At that moment and for no apparent reason, tears welled in her eyes and poured out over her face. Mary buried them away in the pillow, not knowing herself what had caused them and not wanting for a second that Paul should see them and stop. They continued to flow as she cried out into the pillow incoherently, mumbling obscenities based upon her vulgar carnal needs. Her body began to shake uncontrollably as the orgasm took control of her faculties. Her son followed the lead of her body's contractions and rocked deeply in and out of her as the tidal waves of pleasure washed through her womb and out upon his shaft in a musty sweet smelling gush. She lay unable to move, panting heavily as the ecstasy rippled through her like pure voltage.

Paul continued to rock in and out of Mary, softer now that she had crested but enough to make the sensations of orgasm linger into long minutes of inextinguishable fire in her loins. Without warning, her son's hands tightened on her hips as his thick girth jerked sharply inside her vagina, spilling his dangerous seed once again into his own mother's womb. Mary's eyes widened at the feel of his swell within her body. Instinctively, she placed her hand against her belly, feeling almost certain she would feel his cock there flooding her as he ejaculated.

Whether it was because he hadn't made a sound or the fact that she had still been so consumed with her own pleasure, Mary realized that Paul hadn't made a noise when he had climaxed. Instead he gently collapsed against the burning muscles of her moist back and, remaining deeply buried inside her, used his weight to roll them both into a spoon beside each other. Mary shut her eyes as his strong young arms enveloped her and held her against his chest tightly. His heart beat against her spine as they both silently began to breathe a bit more regularly. Her lips curled into a smile as his mouth met the side of her neck. The kisses were delicate and they seeped into her flesh like a small warm blanket against her tingling pores, making the hairs on the back of her neck stand out. As to how Paul could turn off the aggression of such powerful sex and dissolve it so quickly into tenderness, Mary could only wonder and marveled maternally that she had raised such a wonderful man. Any woman would be luckier than she would ever realize with him, and yet there he lay in her bed beside her, holding her as though she were his soul mate. Mary squinted her eyes shut tightly, trying to block out the sudden feeling of love that didn't befit her offspring and she felt she less than deserved.

"Stop being a fool!" She chided herself silently, but the delicious feel of his lips dragging wet kissed down her neck made her internal self abuse seem moot against the flutter of butterflies in her stomach.

"How do you do that? Switch on and off so easily?" She moaned just above a whisper as she stared off towards the window which was rich with condensation again against the chilled morning air outside.

"What do you mean?" Paul whispered back amidst more gentle brushes of his lips against her. Mary took a deep breath, trying to decide on the words that would be least confusing while trying to formulate them in her head in a manner than didn't befuddle her.

"One minute you're fucking me so hard I think my bed will snap and now..." She drifted off as the tingling from her son's mouth distracted her. "Now you hold me and... Paul I've never felt so safe." She explained, certain that the words were making less sense than she'd intended. She wished her son could feel the warmth of feeling in her heart for him. She felt certain it would explain better than she ever was going to be able to. Paul rolled back slightly; his cock withdrawing completely from Mary. At once the heavy wet flood began to spill from her stretched vagina. Everything about the sensation felt incomplete and wanton. She whimpered in protest at the abandoning feeling of emptiness. Paul's firm hand clasped over her shoulder as he pulled her onto her back to face his eyes.

"Mom!" He exclaimed upon seeing the redness around her eyes and the identifiable streaks of tears against her cheeks. "Are you ok?! I hurt you! I'm so sorry!" He blathered in terror. Mary placed her fingers on his lips all too quickly as she shook her head solemnly.

"No baby it wasn't that. To be honest I have no idea why I was crying. That was..." She began, trying to convey how much what had happened meant to her. How he had awoken some primal force inside her; allowed her to be what she had never felt comfortable being with anyone before. "I haven't the words." She finally resigned as Paul looked back at her, suspicious and with eyes that displayed more concern than she felt she deserved. His genuine fear that he had harmed her nearly sent Mary into tears again. "Get a hold of yourself or you're gonna fuck him up even more than you already have!" She tormented herself.

"I'm just..." she tried to rationalize out loud, but realized she had no justifiable explanation for her tears. They had come so suddenly that even she had been unprepared for them.

"You're guilty as sin and you can't admit that to yourself well enough to keep your son out of your cunt!" She thought as she stared into Paul's fearful gaze. She longed to feel one thing or another. The suffering caused by her ever returning shame felt unnatural against the pleasure and desire she felt otherwise.

"It's just crazy female stuff sweetie." She finally lied. Paul looked unconvinced in the extreme. "Middle aged hormones running wild. Really I'm fine, and I assure you the very, very last thing you just did was hurt me." She added, hoping that her playful smile at the reference to their incredibly hot sex would be enough to persuade him. She stared down finally, happy to break eye contact until her gaze relaxed on the long glistening sight of her son's cock, draped over his thigh. Softly, as though trying to make him unaware of it, Mary bit her lip as she fixated on inch after glorious inch of thick skin, still flush with hot blood beneath the surface and saturated in the milky white and clear deposits of both of their heavy orgasms.

"Sure why not?" She chided herself internally. "You may as well; it's not like you can do less damage now." The devil on her shoulder suggested as Mary reached out for Paul's manhood, now lost to her darker needs once more and with all the intention of making sure her little boy didn't leave her bed so messy. "At the very least, it'll get his mind off your emotional masochism." She thought as she started to scoot down the bed to take his dripping cock back into her mouth.

"Isn't this what got us here to begin with this morning?" Paul joked as he lay back, resting his head in his hands and watching Mary brush the tangled train wreck that had become her fiery red hair away from her face and sink his shaft back into her mouth. His tone of voice seemed cocky and sure of itself. A deep satisfied groan grumbled through her lips as she slid them up and down his shaft, suckling the sweet salty breakfast that her vagina had abandoned on him with lewd slurps.

"Fuck..." Paul groaned as he stared down his body at his mother's bobbing head. Her tangled red hair drifted down over hear forehead as she gulped and suckled him and he reached out to brush it back behind her ear, clearly enjoying the spectacle laid out before him. She stared back up at him, crooking her eyebrow up to give her appearance the devilish countenance of some well trained concubine. Paul's head dropped back against a pillow and drifted to the side.

"Shit!" He suddenly exclaimed, forcing Mary to rise up in fear, her heart rising into her throat as though she might see everyone she ever knew standing around her bed staring at her in awe struck disapproval and hatred. Paul's eyes were fixed on her bedside alarm clock. "I was supposed to be at Phil's house half an hour ago!" Paul explained as he began to scramble from the bed. Mary's look was immediately one of shunned disappointment as she remained in the midst of the tossed about mess of linen on her mattress, staring at the spot where Paul had been wondering for a single moment what could possibly be taking him from her so suddenly. Her son stared back down at her, realizing her confusion. "Remember? Phil? Snowboarding?" He explained.

Shattering Mary's befuddled sense of rejection came the distinct memory of the trip Paul was so adamant to leave for. It had after all, been all he had talked about for over a month. Paul's friend Phil was a soldier with no remaining immediate family and on his only leave from his first deployment, had made arrangements with Paul to take a weeklong trip into the Adirondack Mountains to propel themselves down glassy sheets of snow at insane speed for the pure enjoyment of it. Of all of Paul's testosterone fueled athletic enjoyments, snowboarding was the activity that his mother least understood and approved of even less. At the age of 15 he had attempted it for the first time on a school ski trip and had returned to her with a leg broken in two places. Had it not been for the waiver she had personally signed on his behalf, Mary still felt certain the school would have faced a law suit driven solely out of a temporary maternal rage. Despite the outcome however Paul insisted that all he wanted for Christmas that year was his own snow board. Of all the things anyone could admire about her son, he never gave up on anything in his life.

"I remember." She finally replied as she watched Paul vanish from her own room. Down the hall she heard the splash of water collide from the shower nozzle with the tile floor. Shakily, she draped her unsteady legs over the edge of her bed and stood up. The cool dribble of spent ejaculate left inside her seeped out and dripped against her inner thigh. Without thinking she ran her hand between her legs and collected it before running her fingers along her mouth, closing her lips over them in shivering appreciation. "God what's the matter with me?" She whispered as she reached for her robe and drew it tightly over her body as if to hide the shame of her nudity and vulgarity from eyes that were no longer present to stare at her.

Paul's vague outline was easily visible through the shower curtain as Mary entered the bathroom in time to see him lathering his penis to cleanse it of the sticky evidence of their sex. He looked up, taking notice of her presence but continued to wash himself in silence.

"Paul..." Mary began. The doubt had returned; the hampering feeling of wrong doing and fear. Paul looked up at her again and this time held notice of her. "Paul we need to talk about this. And..." Her voice trailed off as the realization of what had to be said hit her with a measurable despair. "And I don't think we should... be together again until we do."

She finally finished. She wanted to run from the room; run from the truth but most of all run from the idea that if they did discuss what they had done and decided it wasn't a good idea to continue that it would never happen again. For all her pain and self loathing at the prospect of being so sick as to corrupt her son's sexuality, Mary had never known the kind of pleasure that she had permitted with him. The water suddenly turned off and Paul pulled the shower curtain aside, the water rippling down his adolescent muscles. He stared at her quietly with no identifiable emotion on his face. Not knowing what he was thinking was bringing Mary close to madness. "I mean... not now obviously. When you come home." She added as if to alleviate any thought Paul might have that he would be any later than he was going to be.

"I know not now Mom." He stated with a smile. "If that's what you want." He nodded as he stepped out and began to towel off.

"I think it's the most sensible thing to do." Mary answered, trying to seem confident in her decision but finding the idea ridiculous since the idea of the sensible and appropriate no longer appeared to apply to their relationship.

"Look I... I have no idea what the hell this is between us." He began. "If someone had told me that this would happen well..." He shrugged silently conveying that he wouldn't have believed it. "I know I don't want it to stop." He added putting extra emphasis on his wishes. "But I don't even really have my head wrapped around how it started. One minute I'm happier than I ever have been and the next..." His voice halted as he searched for the words to explain.

"Sheer panic." Mary finished. Paul nodded in agreement.

"You can't imagine what was going through my mind before I fell asleep last night." He told her as he ran the towel over his cock, magnificent even in its flaccid state. Mary wondered how he had ever grown up in her presence without her noticing it even by accident. A rush of heat spread through her body that she fought to ignore, knowing full well that had he asked it of her, she would have sank to her knees in front of him.

"How did it get so fucked up?" She wondered behind the solemn face of a mother trying to do what was closest to the right thing anymore.

"So yeah, I agree. Let's take this week, think this over and when I come home we'll talk about it." He decided.

"Good." Mary agreed.

"A week." She thought as Paul stepped past her after leaning in and kissing her cheek softly before proceeding to his room down the hall to dress. He seemed to have shut part of himself down, trying forcefully to react as a son. It made Mary uncomfortable. "How the hell am I going to last a week?!" She wondered as she looked over to her side at the fogged up bathroom mirror. She wiped the condensation away to reveal her reflection. The woman that stared back looked like a stranger. Whether that was for better or worse remained to be seen.

Paul collected his bags and Mary walked him to the door.

"I'll be back Friday." He reminded her but it sounded more like reassurance. His face was calm and smiling at her warmly, like a husband would have seemed before leaving for a routine business trip. As he turned from her to grasp the doorknob, Mary reached out to collect his face in her hands, colliding her mouth against his as if to remind him of the thing between them that he had to come home to. The kiss was less than she felt brave enough to offer but more than a mother would ever give. Finally breaking away, she smiled back at him, running her hand over his course facial hair with a scowl.

"Make sure you shave. You're too young to wear a beard." She appraised him, back in mother mode. "Please be careful." She added before kissing him again briefly and allowing him to walk out the door and with him any sense of peace she would feel for seven days. She stared out the living room window until his car peeled away, skidding only a moment on the ice that had formed on the road in the night before turning back around to her empty home. Without really knowing why, Mary immediately made her way back upstairs and discarded her robe. Rifling through her closet, she selected clothes to wear for her morning run and then slipped her shoes on.

As she made her way down the stairs into her foyer, she made a quick detour to the living room and grabbed her purse. Seven days wasn't likely to pass quickly without someone to talk to and she knew it. Rummaging until she found her iphone, she stroked the screen to life and selected her contacts list, scanning through until Samantha's name came into view. Mary hesitantly clicked the text message icon beside it.

Her fingers danced around the electronic keyboard.

Her pulse had quickened noticeably and it seemed forever to complete the seven simple key entries. Pausing for a moment, Mary took a deep breath as she held her thumb over the glowing green send icon, knowing all too well the flood gate she was about to unleash. Abandoning her last bit of common sense she finally tapped down and watched the icon that meant the message was going through circle around tauntingly before vanishing, and with it, Mary's last hope of keeping her deeds to herself. She stared down at the phone until the backlight faded and the screen blinked off altogether. In truth, Mary was amazed no series of frenzied replies had already prompted the cell to chime without end. Never the less as she held it in her hand it sat motionless and silent. Shrugging her shoulders in dismissal, she finally tossed it back into her purse, threw her arms into her jacket and stepped outside her front door into the harsh winter morning to escape in the indulgence of the only thing in her day that was likely to feel normal.

The street was near silent with only one car passing her house as she moved down her driveway towards the snowy pavement. The familiar face of a neighbor behind it's wheel shot her a wave as he passed and she smiled superficially in reply. Mary appraised the conditions carefully as she pulled her heart monitor out of her shorts and strapped it over her wrist. Lately, the plows that moved through the neighborhood had done a lousy job of clearing the streets and she had avoided them for safety reasons, favoring instead the long stretch of hand shoveled sidewalk that she and the neighbors maintained throughout New York's blustery winters. This morning however the road seemed passable enough and she shot off into a run opposite the direction the car had come from.

This was her time. Running had become Mary's escape from life many years ago when a friend had suggested fitness as a means to vent stress. No matter what was going on in her world, the road had always been there. Its black surface had always stared up at her with no judgment and no opinions. Some people drank and others smoked. Others had even more self destructive habits that they validated as their way to escape life and find a moments peace. Mary ran. Her quick pace rounded her through miles of interconnected housing developments. The houses around her, white and silent went by in a steady blur of peripheral vision as she focused ahead. Her mind was quiet and her heart steady. Her toned legs confidently beat the toes of her tennis shoes into the thin crunch of thin snow beneath them. Her red hair trailed behind her as she glided forward. She rarely tied it up when she ran, favoring instead to let the wind catch it and cool her head. Despite the whipping arctic wind in the air, Mary's exposed skin glistened in the late morning sunlight, heavy with all the grimy saturation a good workout had to offer. She slowed to a walk, as she approached her home again, breathing in heavily the icy air around her as she cocked her wrist upward and stared at the heart monitor to evaluate her rapid pulse. She groaned in spite of herself. It had been a Christmas gift from Paul the previous year, and now it had become a reminder that when she opened her front door he wouldn't be home and as yet, things remained far less resolved than she would have liked. The escape was over. She looked back at the road and silently thanked it for the hour of relief it had once again given her.

Mary's porch was a treacherous sheet of ice under her feet as she dug her house key out of her windbreaker and slid it into the deadbolt. Silently, she made a mental note to salt the porch as she eagerly pushed the door open and collapsed her back against it once inside to shut out the chill which had already begun to sap the energy from her as the heat of her body dwindled. Not sooner than she had crossed the foyer and into the kitchen and no later than she had freed one arm from her jacket came the familiar chime of her phone, distant though it was in the next room and buried in the clutter of her handbag. Mary hoped to find her son's name as a text or even a missed call, but she knew it wasn't realistic. By then Paul was close to being on a mountainside with Phil, flying moronically down a black diamond on a ridged piece of fiberglass. Clumsily, she dug her hand into the purse until it found her phone and she tapped the screen as she patted her forehead dry with a kitchen towel.

"Good lord!" Mary exclaimed aloud as her eyes widened to absorb the sight of multiple texts and no less than a dozen missed calls, all bearing Samantha's name beside them. Unwillingly, Mary tapped open the texts to read them.

Read the last of the messages. Each seemed to be raising their voice at Mary as she silently read them over. Switching back to the missed calls, she laughed a little at Samantha's persistence. Each was not more than three minutes in separation from the next. Before she could tap one to reply to however the phone roared to life again with Sam's name above the incoming call icon. Mary breathed a short laugh and answered.

"Hello?" She chimed merrily as if to make light of an onslaught of incoming frustration.

"Hello my ass! Where have you been? I've called you a hundred times!" Samantha replied with an exasperated tone. If words could take form and reach through the phone, Mary felt certain she would be on the floor with Samantha's hands at her throat.

"I noticed. I went out for a run." She replied. Her friend let out a noticeably lengthy huff of air that crackled in Mary's receiver.

"My understanding of how you can do that when it's negative ten degrees outside aside, you can't drop a bomb like that on me and then just... not be there!" Samantha scolded.

"I'm sorry I..." Mary began.

"Yeah yeah yeah..." Samantha interrupted, obviously in no mood to dwell on it further. "Now what do you mean did it?"

Mary's voice stalled out in her throat. It was as though the next words that were going to come from her mouth weren't supposed to belong to her. Swallowing hard to compose herself she finally broke the pause.

"I... Paul and I... we made love last night." She replied so quietly she expected her friend to ask her to speak up and repeat herself. The air on the other end of the phone however was uncomfortably silent for several seconds.

"I'm coming over." Samantha answered at last.

"Sam I just got back in; I need a shower and..." Mary began. It was true, but she had to admit the excuse she was trying to formulate was a distant second to her lack of desire to get into the gritty details she was certain Samantha would demand before she had provided herself ample time enough to sort them out for herself.

"Leave your door unlocked. I'm already getting in my car." Samantha replied in dismissal. True to her words, Mary vaguely swore she heard the sound of an engine turning over in the background before the line curtly went dead. Mary took the phone from her ear and scanned her eyes across the 'call ended' status screen that had appeared. With a wary eye, she stared up the street through the living room window, almost certain to see Samantha's red Mitsubishi Eclipse tearing towards her house with a contrail of scattered snow and burnt rubber trailing behind it in close pursuit.

Deciding that she would deal with Samantha when that time came, Mary turned on her heals and walked back upstairs to the bathroom. The sink top and mirror were still damp with the heat of Paul's shower. Mary kicked her shoes off as she pulled the nozzle against the tile wall. The shower head spattered with complaint as it forced hot water through the cold pipes in the walls before unleashing its torrent. Undressing, Mary ignored the bathroom mirror and any opportunity to see her sinful side stare back at her.

The water sizzled against her flesh as she stepped into the tub and pulled the curtain closed after her. The temperature was hotter than she preferred. It was Paul's usual custom to boil his skin from his bones when he bathed. Mary had grown accustomed over the years to adjusting the temperature down a bit before stepping in after he had occupied the bathroom first. With everything on her mind however, she had simply forgotten this time and quickly reached down to turn the chrome dial before she cooked like a lobster. Once she was more comfortable, she reached towards her lavender body wash but paused as her hand stilled in front of Paul's blue and black bottle of Axe Phoenix. Not knowing why, she grabbed it instead and squeezed a liberal amount onto her bath sponge. The entire room filled with her son's scent as she ran the soap over her skin slowly, closing her eyes and selfishly envisioning him against her. The aroma triggered torrid images of his mouth along her body and the feel of him harshly penetrating her. Her mind drifted into the dangerous place it had come from again as she imagined him pulling her down to his waiting gorgeous body laying in the bathtub; his erect cock sinking up into her as she straddled him and the hot water cascading down her back. Mary's legs trembled unsteadily at the thought.

"It's going to be a long damn week." She whispered to herself.

Opening her eyes, she shook the fantasy off like a cold chill and proceeded to finish washing off as quickly as possible. Grabbing her hair in her fingers, she rounded it under her nose and decided that there was no need to wash it and turned towards the showerhead to rinse the sponge clean of the musky masculine soap before shutting the water off altogether and stepping out into the steamy haze of the bathroom. After patting her plush towel over her skin, she wrapped it around her slender body and then pulled her hair back into a pony tail with a brown scrunchie she kept by the sink and walked back down the hall into her bedroom and opened the door to her spacious walk-in closet.

"Feel better?" A voice chimed unexpectedly from behind her. Mary's heart leapt into her throat as she jumped nearly a foot into the air. Whipping around so fast the towel spread open and nearly fell from her body, she stared at her bed where Samantha lay on her side smiling at her.

"Jesus Christ, Sam!" Mary groaned as she placed her hand against her chest to quell her racing heart from breaking through the skin. "I didn't see you there. You scared the crap out of me." She whispered and regarded her friend with an unkind look. Samantha simply beamed back at her. It was at that moment that Mary took notice of the pile of linen next to her bed and saw that her best friend was lying on a bare mattress.

"Did you strip my bed for me?" Mary asked a little befuddled. Samantha laughed and looked around her.

"Three out of four pillows on the floor, the mattress sheet hanging on by a corner, the rest all crumpled up and erratic in the bottom corner of the bed; sweetie I'd say you did a good enough job stripping it yourself." She chided with a playful grin. Mary again regarded her friend with a less than pleasant countenance as she shook her head and pulled the haphazard towel off of her moist skin to return to her closet for a change of clothes. She wasn't sure why but she felt awkwardly certain that Samantha was staring at her harder now that she was naked.

"So was there something wrong with the couch downstairs?" Mary complained aloud, evidently still flustered by the shock of her friends intrusion into her bedroom as she tugged a sweater over her head.

"Scene of the crime; how could a girl resist?" Samantha explained as she ran her hand over the mattress like she was touching a luxurious fur rug.

"Thank you." Mary turned and scolded. "As if I don't feel enough like a horrible person, let's just get a criminal shot in there." She added before turning to her dresser to fish out a pair of comfortable jeans.

"Oh please. You know I didn't mean it like that. It's a figure of speech." Samantha justified.

"It was a shitty choice of words is what it was Sam." Mary replied without an upward glance as she stepped her feet one after the other into the pants and tugged them over her shapely hips.

"You know, if you are planning on anyone else coming over today you might want to spray some Febreze in here. I could smell your room from the base of the stairs Char." Samantha went on, oblivious to Mary's disgruntled reactions. Her friend pretended to ignore her as she dug through another drawer for socks. "... Smells like a whorehouse." Samantha added jokingly, causing Mary to whip her head in her direction with a ferocious stare that silenced and stilled Sam's playful taunts and demeanor.

"Why did I text you again?" Mary asked rhetorically. Samantha popped off the bed and walked over to her, wrapping her arms around Mary's body and pulling her into a tight hug.

"Because you need a friend and I'm just being an ass. I'm sorry. I'm just a little excited to hear about this and I'm being sarcastic." She answered before letting Mary go. Her attitude had noticeably changed back to something less obnoxious.

"No I'm sorry." Mary sighed. "I'm just... I don't know what I am Sam." Mary rubbed her forehead in her hands before looking back up at her friends with a weak smile. "You want some coffee?" She suggested, trying to see if it was possible to take the mood of the conversation in a different direction.

"I brought wine." Sam piped up with a smile.

"Sam, it's 11:30 in the morning." Mary observed after glancing at her alarm clock. Her heart sank in her chest. "Stupid clock. Thanks to you I'm alone for a week." She thought and smiled at her own silliness to blame a clock for the fact that it would be seven whole days until she could reach some measure of understanding with Paul or at least some measure of closure depending on the direction their decisions lead them. Samantha grabbed her by the wrist and began pulling her out into the hall.

"Fine. You talk and I'll drink." She stated flatly, leading Mary down the stairs and into her living room where she tossed her haphazardly onto the couch and crashed beside her. "Crap! Wine! Sorry my head's in a million places right now." She scoffed as she bounced off the couch and crossed the room to her obscenely large purse and produced a bottle of merlot that despite the handbags size, Mary found it odd that it should fit inside. "Glasses?" Sam asked while making her way into the kitchen. Mary shook her head in amusement.

"Top left, lush." She replied without looking up. A minute later Samantha came bounding back into the living room with the uncorked bottle and two wine glasses.

"Brought you one too in case you change your mind." Her voice rang as she got comfortable in the corner of the sofa. Mary simply shook her head in the negative but Samantha hardly noticed as she was already pouring a generous helping for herself. After sipping down a quarter of the glass in a single attempt, she finally set it down on Mary's oak coffee table and stared back with her full attention.

"So..." Sam began.

"Yeah..." Mary sighed, her eyes drifting to the floor that had no more ability to judge her than the road before and yet she still felt like there may have been some way that everything in the house had eyes to what she had done. "If these walls could talk, I'd be in jail." She thought to herself.

"Oh come on!" Samantha urged impatiently with a rousing shake against Mary's thigh. "You can't not tell me what happened." Her voice was nearly whining.

"I told you already. I did it." Mary answered, knowing full well her companion would in no way be satisfied to leave it at that. She looked up from the rug at Samantha's annoyed face. "What? What am I supposed to say? I fucked my own son, I'm a terrible mother and an even worse person and, and..." Her voice trailed off. She might have begun to cry again if her eyes hadn't already had enough recent exercise.

"Did it go... badly?" Sam asked, leaning in with genuine concern on her face. Mary couldn't help it; the explosion of laughter that erupted from her lips was hearty and almost maniacal. Sam crooked an eyebrow up at her hysterical friend in bewilderment, but allowed Mary to purge the distressed emotion in whatever manner she needed to until she calmed down again.

"Badly..." She repeated. "It was the most incredible thing I have ever experienced." She confessed in a faint whisper and then returned her eyes to the floor. Mary nearly expected Sam's arms to come flying around her again and a torrent of personal questions and demands for all the slimy details to ensue. Samantha however remained quite still with a noticeable measure of attempted control and simply looked back at her friend so calmly Mary felt like she was lying on a psychiatrist's sofa.

"Do you want to talk about it?" She finally asked before grasping her wine glass again and taking another copious swallow.

"I wouldn't know how to start." Mary confessed. Once again the memories of her actions came back to her vividly only now they were a jumble; out of order and one piling into the other in a heap of crazed emotional distress.

"Just, start at the beginning. How it stared... and go from there if you want to. I'll just listen." She promised. Her voice felt comforting. Mary situated herself more comfortably on the sofa facing Samantha and began to recall the events of the previous day as she remembered them. Her friend sat attentively next to her, staying quiet as promised. Mary felt if hard to look her in the eye as she described making love to Paul; the passion despite the shame. The overwhelming fulfillment coupled with the turmoil of her ethics. Despite the tingling intensity of her recollections, the blend of sin and perfect contentment still battled for dominance inside her. Not until she had finished filling Sam in on the events that ended the night before did she take a break in the tale long enough for her confidant to feel comfortable interjecting.

"And... what? All that happened and this morning he just left you to go skiing?" Samantha asked. Her voice sounded irritated as though she was supporting Mary in some unsaid disapproval that Paul would throw his mother a 'hit it and quit it'.

"Snowboarding." She corrected before shaking her head. "And no... actually I'm not finished." She added to the wide eyed disbelief of Samantha who sat back in her place on the couch and prepared herself for the story to continue. Taking a deep breath, Mary went on to explain what had taken place after she awakened next to Paul; how she had been unable to control her impulses and what it had lead to as well as the justifiable cause of Paul's abrupt departure. This time Samantha's calmness steadily dissolved into obvious excitement. She fidgeted in place as though bursting to interrupt but remained, much to Mary's relief, quiet and attentive as she let her finish.

"So you see... it's not like he just bailed on me." Mary defended Paul. "He'd been planning this trip for a while and..."

Samantha held a hand up in dismissal, having taken a new stance on Paul's vanishing act than her previous assumption. Mary sat quietly, awaiting a more outrageous reaction from her friend. Samantha simply grabbed the bottle of wine and filled both glasses and handed one to Mary despite her earlier refusal.

"Here's to the two of you." She stated happily as she tapped her glass against Mary's and tossed more merlot down her throat before setting hers down on the table again. "I am so jealous I can't begin." She beamed.

"Sam seriously." Mary chided, setting her glass down on the table without any interest. "You're acting like a just told you I was engaged. I don't even know if this is going to continue. It shouldn't right? It can't!"

"Why not?" Sam asked. "Who knows? I mean aside from me of course and it's not like I would ever tell anyone." She added. Her voice had returned to some of its earlier giddiness.

"It's insane!" Mary shouted outrageously. "Forgetting the moral reasons if I can for a moment, what can I possibly hope to expect from this in the future. Paul is 18 years old. He's going to college soon; obviously he'll eventually meet someone..." She rambled.

"Oh so that's what this is about." Samantha interrupted. "You are afraid of being replaced."

"What? No! I'm simply saying that even if I could come to a point where my guilt wasn't in the way anymore sooner or later..."

"Hang on right there." Samantha interrupted again. "What's stopping you?"

"What do you mean?" Mary replied, taken out of her rant in confusion.

"What's stopping you from coming to that point? The one where your guilt isn't in the way anymore." Sam asked.

"Paul and I haven't talked and..." Mary tried to explain.

"Exactly. You two haven't talked. And you need to talk to each other before you can make all these assumptions and conclusions Char. Otherwise, Paul is going to come home in seven days and you will have worked yourself up into such a frenzy asking yourself these questions that you have no answers to and you will have already made the decision to end a wonderful thing without him and he's going to resent you for that." Samantha cautioned with a stern tone. Mary sat blankly looking at her friend who had just made a surprising amount of sense.

"You have to calm down Char. I swear I will never underestimate your uncanny ability to over think yourself into a heart attack and it's always led you into making choices you wished later you could unmake; for as long as I've known you. You have to take this week to remember what was so incredible about being with him or you're just going to make a rash choice alone." She added, reaching for Mary's wine glass again and planting it in her friend's hand. Mary looked down at the burgundy merlot for a long moment, letting Sam's advice sink in before shrugging her shoulders and placing the glass to her lips. It went down easy with a warm embrace that soothed the tension that had formed throughout her body.

"It was... absolutely incredible." She finally said with a longing tone of voice.

"I'll say." Her friend chimed with a ear to ear smile. "My panties are like the inner wall of the Hoover fucking dam!" She added breaking into delirious laughter as she collapsed back onto her back along the sofa like a child at a sleep over talking about boys. If Mary hadn't known better, she could easily have envisioned pajamas and a pillow fight in her future. "What?" Samantha asked, appraising Mary's look of stand offish amusement. "I'm telling you I'm jealous. The way you described being with him was the hottest shit I've heard in forever! I swear if I had half of your bravery..." Her voice trailed off as she bit her lip seductively and grinned.

"Glad I could entertain you." Mary sighed. "Seriously Sam, am I crazy?"

"Certifiably." Samantha answered happily before finishing her glass and setting it back down. "But I guess that means they'd have to lock us both up and I for one think you are the luckiest girl alive." She declared to Mary's puzzlement. "I have fantasies about my son so hot they keep me awake at night and you actually got to know what it's like. Twice! You said that you had never felt so fulfilled. If that's crazy hand me a straight jacket cause I'll take it." She affirmed with a finality of thought that indicated she wouldn't likely have anything negative to say on the matter.

"It's terrifying." Mary whispered.

"The best things in life usually always are at first." Sam replied.

CHAPTER 3

"Oh God. Not again." Mary grumbled in disgrace as the rays of morning light stabbed between her eyelids that seemed less than willing to completely open. Her hand, still buried in her underwear, felt overly warm and betrayed the moisture between her thighs as she rubbed her slick fingertips together. For the third morning in a row since her son Paul had left her house, she had awakened from torrid dreams of their incestuous revelations to the realization that her body had demanded more than unconscious recollection in her dreams. Her clitoris still pulsed with the stimulation she had only just abandoned upon waking and the sensation coursed through her body with a terrible need to culminate in climax.

In the dawning moments of consciousness, the visions of her dreams; that of her son between her over eagerly parted legs, sinking his blessed manhood into her sex over and over, still felt as real as the room around her was becoming and without much care to invite reality too early, Mary sank her fingers back where her body needed them still. The renewed splendor of penetration sent her ecstasy into sharper relief and she rolled over onto her back, pulling one of her shapely legs up under her other arm to make her labors easier. Her breathing began to rasp as her hand darted between her legs with its own will, sending her fingertips into her shuddering wetness with decadent enthusiasm.

"God baby, harder..." She whispered, already half way back into the dream of Paul's cock sinking in and out of her, his own mother, the depraved whore such as she had become for him, longing to fulfill a need that seemed now rather boundless. Despite her shame she craved his body against hers, but the protection that her solitude provided allowed her to continue without much reflection on morality. The lust had once again taken control, replacing Mary's higher reasoning with the carnal needs that she fought daily now to restrict within herself. What had begun to trouble her most however, was the fact that each time she submitted to her furtive lusts, her body seemed to require more to satiate its appetite. Her fingers felt inadequate, measured against the memory of Paul's cock filling her as no man's had before. Mary dropped her leg alongside the other, the burning in her core demanding more to be quenched.

"This has gotten out of hand!" She thought with aggravation, but too much had been done for her loins to allow her to stop now. Mary rolled to her side, reaching desperately for her night stand as the beast within her screamed like a starving wolf at the moon. The drawer yanked open too easily, nearly spilling its contents onto the carpet beside her bed as Mary grasped and discarded a book and her reading glasses case before her fingers wrapped around the shaft of the phallic instrument of pleasure that she hoped desperately would calm the storm in her loins. With trembling hands she twisted the base switch until the toy vibrated to life on its most forceful setting. She stared at it a moment, singing its rhythmic song in her hands, wishing for a moment that if she were to slide it into her mouth it would bear the flavor of her son's salty skin.

Rolling over again, she penetrated herself before she was even settled, her inner walls pulsing with the dildo's playful dance. Harshly she worked it in and out, grunting lewdly and without care as she imagined again being taken with the tremendous force she now only imagined her son inflicting on her. Her eyes had slammed shut, replacing her surroundings with the fantasy of Paul's hands pinning her knees back against her heavy breasts. She could see him, beautiful and young, thrusting his hips forward until every inch of his penis vanished between her sensitive labia. He was strong; his eyes determined. She was his again; damn all her inner resistance, she would forever be his as long as he was inside her. She could decide if she hated herself for it later.

Mary gasped out incoherently, the sound of her whispers and moans accompanies only by the low dull buzz of her toy and the coaxed juiciness seeping from her womb. The images in her mind altered, taking her body involuntarily with them. Without a care for the effort of it, Mary rolled over onto her stomach, panting into her pillow as she raised her bottom up. The blanket slid from her body exposing her thong clad sex to the ceiling before she tore the saturated underwear down the back of her thighs and sank the toy back inside her inconsolable vagina from behind.

"Fuck yes!" Mary screamed as she crammed it forcefully against her g-spot. A flash of how obscene she had to look occurred to her in that desperate moment of sexual need and weakness; ass in the air and one hand reached around to penetrate herself as though Paul himself were in her bed where she needed him, grasping her waist, calling her his and taking her for his pleasure.

"Paul... Paul!" She groaned repetitively as she relentlessly besieged her swollen vagina to batter against the spot that promised absolute release.

"God Paul, fuck me to death! I'm cumming!" Mary screamed as her muscles tightened around the toy in jarring grips before dispensing a spastic feminine ejaculation that brought her slumping down flat against her belly once more. Her hand released the toy in exhaustion and it continued to pulsate, unguided in the depths of her quivering wetness. The climax had overpowered her to the brink of exhaustion. It felt without end of depth and relentlessness as it tore through her body with a tsunami of breath stealing pleasure. Even when, after some time, the toy buzzed its way free of her body and danced in the wet spot left on her sheets between her trembling thighs, Mary made no dare to move and disrupt the ebb and flow of internal bliss that frenzied through her nerves. Only until the moment had fully passed, and the fantasy fully faded away; only when the buzzing phallus had begun to annoyingly knock against the side of her knee did she roll to her side, turn it off and toss it off the bed before letting her composure return to her enough to competently sit up and scoot her underwear back up her hips. The coolness of her own moisture on the fabric, long removed from her body to freely interact with the chilly air of the room, pressed against her clitoris and sent one last lingering current through her core.

The beast within was silent now, asleep until her immoral cravings awakened it again. Its less pleasant counterpart took its place in her thoughts, riddling Mary with guilt and indignity as she reluctantly stood up and moved towards her dresser, in her daily mindless routine to select attire in which to exercise. With self disgust she pulled the tainted thong back off again and helplessly rubbed it against her vagina, only slightly less than horrified at how much of her dampness had smeared across it before tossing the garment in her laundry basket and slipping a fresh pair back up her legs. After donning a pair of her insulated black running pants and a purple tank top, Mary turned to face the disarray that she had once again made of her bed. Her pillows were scattered and the thick down comforter had been kicked into one corner of the mattress and lay half on the floor. In the center of the linen, like a testament to her corruption was the large dark stain the size of a dinner plate and several scattered smears of saturation that her toy had done the honor of dribbling around her bed before she had found the ability to move and shut it off. With a sigh that felt too heavy for her own lungs, Mary grabbed at a corner of the bedding to peel it free of the mattress and add it to her inundated thong in the laundry before she stopped short, staring at the clutter like it was a task far larger than it really was.

"Screw it." She huffed and let loose of the fabric in frustration. Her mind was in too many places to play the domesticated woman and she crossed her room around her bed, promising herself that she'd take care of it after a hard run and a well earned shower. As she flung her curtains open however, all good intentions dissolved to the depressing sight of snow falling so thick, Mary had to squint through it to make out the house across the street. What should have been a view of the road below her was masqueraded in thick sparkling white. The distinction between elevation of the street and the shouldering curbs was gone and the more she stared, Mary felt certain it had been surpassed by several feet of frozen precipitation. Cars parked in their driveways were submerged to their side mirrors and for all the chaos before her eyes, it was apparent that the city snow plows had not even bothered to begin any attempt to start their efforts in her neighborhood.

"Punishment, right?" Mary asked as she stared upward out the frosty pane at her faceless and seemingly mocking creator concealed behind heavy cloud cover, before slouching her shoulders in defeat and turning back towards her dresser, kicking her running pants off as she moved and flicking them with her foot onto her bed with the lump of musty sweet smelling linen. After sliding a heavy pair of sweatpants back on, she snatched up the dildo from is discarded location on her rug. It glistened with the saturation of extended use, but rather than provide Mary with the smile of satisfaction that it had done its duty admirably, it had become another token symbolizing her feelings of utter failure as a mother. Hurriedly, she rounded the corner from her bed room, making her way to the sink in her bathroom where she thrust the robotic phallus under hot running water and began to wipe it clean with a hand towel with a mania an onlooker might confuse with a person destroying evidence of some horrid crime. When the dildo once again had adopted all of the clean normalcy that a sex toy possibly could, she walked back into her room, tossed it in her bedside drawer amidst a clutter of condoms and ball point pens and slammed it shut as though she couldn't have been happier to have it out of sight.

The walk down the slender flight of stairs to her living room seemed to Mary to be a decent into Hell as she knew she would be unable to look upon her sofa without vivid images of her son gripping his masculinity with all the splendor of its engorged potential in a full color flashback of what had started everything she now resented herself for. Trying not to look at its now innocent appearance, she sank into its soft cushions and grabbed for the television remote, giving little notice to the growling in her stomach begging for breakfast. Her thumb tapped the channel control rapidly as her eyes masterfully surveyed passing programs that, in the blink of a second displayed nothing interesting to force her to linger there.

"Can't run; nothing on TV..." Mary huffed with irritation. "This should be a fun day." She added as she rolled back off the couch, punched in the numerals on the remote for the weather channel and walked into her kitchen.

"...an absolutely awful storm." A meteorologist's voice trailed off as Mary opened her refrigerator and dug around for a Tupperware container filled with freshly chopped melon that she had cut up the night before. As she grabbed a fork out of another drawer and flipped the switch on her coffee maker the television spoke again forcing her attention back towards the living room.

"If you're just joining us, we direct your attention to the north eastern section of New York where something of a small blizzard is consuming the North Country." The announcer chimed more merrily than such circumstances deserved. Mary plopped back into the couch and began to eat as she stared at the man on the screen who was wearing what, for all Mary could account, seemed to be a suit made out of motel drapes. He was circling his hand against the digital image of an enormous storm that was sweeping over her area and worse, towards Paul's. Instinctively she set down her tub of melon and hunched over the arm of the couch, wiggling her fingers into her handbag which was just out of reach to make it an uncomfortable stretch until she found her phone. Not bothering to settle back into place first, she tapped the screen to life. No icons stood out indicating missed calls, texts or voicemails. Mary pulled herself back up into place and once again eyed her television. The animation being displayed confirmed her fears. A large dark purple oval that was presently right on top of her town was being shown drifting towards the right and resting comfortably over where her son was probably already racing down white slopes with little intention of moving on after.

"Crap..." Mary cursed meagerly, and then smiled in spite of herself as it occurred to her that her concern for Paul was the first thought she had had about him all morning which hadn't panged her with guilt. As soon as the warmth of that simple pleasure was through her, her mind betrayed its darker ambitions, replacing her maternal instinct with baser needs for him to come home safely. The animal in her loins grumbled in its sleep.

"Put the phone down Mary." She said to herself, and obeying her own better sense she set it down in her lap and stared back at the television without really taking into account what she was seeing before her. Her head was starting to swim with the prospect of his presence and the closure it might bring them. Her eyes settled back into her lap at the calm black screen of her iphone which stared back as though flat out daring her to pick it up.

"No." She thought. "Let him be. You're a mess and he'll know it if you call." As she set the phone back down on the arm of the couch drumming her fingers against her hip in anxiety as she tried to concentrate on the television.

"And as you can see here on the DOPLAR, the storm system will continue to gust down from Canada and into the northern and northeastern areas of New York, bringing with it significant lake effect snow and high wind. Temperatures in the Adirondack areas are expected to drop into the low teens and well into the negatives by evening with snow accumulation of five feet or more by nine o'clock tonight. Residents are advised to avoid travel if and at all possible and certainly to avoid major highways after 7pm." The weather man reported as Mary stared intently at the dark purple highlight of the RADAR behind the reporter as it repeated it's animation; resting finally over the precise area that her son was staying. She glanced back down at her phone and back to the television. Deciding that a call from a concerned parent could be made to sound less needy than she felt, Mary picked her phone back up, highlighted her son's name in her list and tapped it. Her arm felt shaky as she tucked her hair behind her ear and lifted the cell to it.

"Relax." She exhaled as the ringtone chimed. A mere several seconds of rings felt like an eternity as she fidgeted deeper into her place on the sofa.

"Hi Mom." Paul's deep voice sounded in Mary's ear as soon as the line clicked over. Hearing it sent a current through her body that was anything but maternal.

"Hi Paul. I'm watching the news and the weather heading for your area..." She began, her voice cracking so nervously that she felt like she was back in middle school, calling a boy for the first time. "Well... how's the weather out there anyhow?" She finished meekly.

"How's the weather? You did not just say that." She scolded herself, cupping her forehead in her hand in silent embarrassment. For all her preconceived notions about how nervous she was, Mary realized that there wasn't going to be any way to escape the call without making a fool of herself. Fighting every urge to simply hang up and blame it on poor signal, she pressed the phone against her ear more firmly and braced herself for more of the same flutter her nerves would provide when her son spoke to her again.

"I imagine it's every bit as bad as the TV says it is." Paul replied with a casual voice. In the distance, Mary heard many voices moving in and out of her son's vicinity. "We're all packed into the lodge right now hoping for a break but it doesn't look like we're gonna get one." He added.

"It's really coming down huh? Same here. In fact from what I'm seeing, you haven't even gotten the worst of it yet." Mary replied hopelessly.

"Stop talking about the weather or get off the phone you moron!" Her embarrassment shouted in her mind. Mary swallowed hard, searching into the recesses of her memory for a time not long passed when having a simple conversation with her son was still a relatively easy occurrence.

"Terrific. Well we were expecting as much. It's already bad enough out here that they won't let us on the slopes." Paul replied with defeat in his tone. The air on the phone went quiet between them as Mary moved her lips silently hoping with each passing second that the connection between them would fail so that she could stop trying to think of something to say. "Is everything alright? Did I lose you?" Paul asked, his voice changing to one of concern.

"No I'm fine here." Mary lied. "Actually I was more concerned about you out there."

"Well, we may have to take off earlier than expected so we don't get snowed in here." Paul remarked before saying something under his breath to someone close by him. Mary couldn't make it out and wasn't really interested anyhow. The simple idea that her son might have to return to her early spread like a wave of warm hope that permeated all the inappropriate areas her body had to offer. She looked out the living room window at the blizzard burying her mailbox and silently prayed that it continue.

"Oh. Well of course if you need to come home..." She began but stopped short, hearing the happiness in her voice that shouldn't have been there. "That is to say, I don't want you getting stuck or worse; into an accident. You scare the hell out of me whenever you take your car out in the snow to begin with." She continued, feeling proud that she had managed to come across at least in part, more like a mother than an optimistic girlfriend. "You'll keep me posted right?"

"Yeah of course." Paul answered through the crackle of failing reception.

"Is everything else alright? Are you coming home in one piece?" Mary asked. "How is Phil doing? Everything ok there?" She asked, hearing her words dissolve into a blather of disjointed nonsense.

"Alright woman. How about one question at a time before he doesn't want to come home to your babbling ass at all?" She scolded herself unremittingly, feeling more hopeless with each syllable that came out of her mouth.

"Um yeah, I'm fine. Phil's fine; everything's fine. Mom, are you sure you're ok?" Her son replied. Mary silently cursed, knowing full well what had prompted such a question. She closed her eyes, breathing deeply to regain composure. Her heart was pounding in her chest and for all the chill coming through the window next to her, she felt like she was steadily becoming feverish.

"I... miss you." She finally said just above a whisper into the receiver of her phone which felt heavier in her hand with each passing second. She wondered if Paul understood the context that her words were meant to convey. Gritting her teeth, Mary waited for the reply to the simple truth she had not intended to express when she had dialed him up.

"I miss..." Paul began and then stopped short. Mary tore the phone from her ear to check the call status on the phone, dreadfully fearful the conversation had been dropped, before replacing it against her head. "I want to say I miss you too but..." He said, stopping again. Mary's desperation peaked into verbal machine gun fire.

"No! I meant... Paul I meant that I just miss you. You know? In a 'mom' way? I wasn't trying to force anything. I'm sorry. I didn't want to make you uncomfortable. I didn't want..." She rambled with terror in her tone.

"You did it!" She chided herself. "You pushed too fast and you've freaked him out! You freaked him out and nothing's going to ever be the same!" Mary ranted internally as she folded her knees up to bounce her forehead off of.

"Mom! Give me a second ok? I'm just not in the best place to... just hold on a second, ok?" Paul replied with exasperation.

"Yeah." She whispered as a tear ran down her cheek. She listened in the phone at the scuffle of changing sounds and background noise for nearly an eternal minute before her son returned.

"You still there?" Paul asked. The air around him had grown nearly silent.

"Yes." She answered; her voice still unable to rise above a whisper, though she realized that he had relocated because it was he who could not talk without ears all around to hear him.

"I was going to say I miss you too..." Paul began again. "But it wasn't the right word." He finished, motivating Mary to lift her head from its drooped resting place against her knees. "Mom I literally haven't had a second to myself since I left where you weren't on my mind." He concluded. The panic that had so quickly consumed Mary fled, replaced by the flutter of a butterfly with A.D.D. in her stomach. "And I've gone in and out of being so hot for you that I've nearly bailed on Phil a hundred times, to staring at myself in the mirror, wondering what the hell we've done." He finished. Like a weight lifted, Mary lay back on her sofa smiling widely at the relieved burden of believing she was the only one who felt so lost. Despite any motherly desire that her son was away, enjoying himself apart from the cares of life, there was a selfish happiness in that perhaps, she was not the only one teetering on the brink of madness.

"Paul I'm a wreck." She confessed. "Part of me wants to tell you how sorry I am for this. Another part..." She paused trying to decide whether to finish the thought. "... Wants you home so I can tear your clothes off." She admitted, deciding that she would probably communicate more effectively if she abandoned the pretenses under which she had called. The truth felt better.

"Hang on a second Mom." Paul replied. The sudden silence on his end was replaced with a flurry of muttered voices that Mary couldn't distinguish despite how intently she listened. Each moment they weren't talking felt like a tap of water between her eyes that was steadily robbing her of her sanity.

"Mom the resort is closing down completely on account of the storm cause the weatherman said this isn't gonna let up for a couple of days. Phil and I just agreed that the fun's over. I'm coming home." Paul sighed.

"Really?!" Mary gasped, before realizing that she probably sounded too enthused about her son's misfortune. "And when you get home we'll... we'll talk right?" She added hopefully.

"In this weather I might not be able to get home till late." Paul answered. Mary grew suddenly worried, hoping that his words were more a statement of fact and not an effort to postpone the inevitable.

"I want to talk. We need to talk Paul. I have no problem staying up as late as it takes." She answered, pleased at how resolute she seemed to sound.

"Then we'll talk." He affirmed back to her. "Listen Mom, Phil and I need to get our stuff loaded up in the cars and get out of here fast. We're not the only one's leaving and the road is gonna be bad enough without a hundred people trying to get out of here."

"Go sweetie." Mary replied. "I promise I'll still be up when you get in and for the love of God, drive carefully."

"Love you." Paul replied, and the line clicked dead leaving Mary feeling vacant in the hole his absence left behind.

"I love you too Paul, so much." Mary whispered as she pulled the phone from her ear and stared outside again. The snowflakes had grown noticeably larger and tapped against the window pane like little white pieces of cork. Across the street and barely visible through a static of white, neighbors were already scrambling out of their warm homes all bundled up in thick coats and knit caps to shovel driveways and brush off cars in the futile hope that it would make a difference. Mary had lived in the north country too long not to know better and pulled the quilt she kept over the back of her sofa down over her body and snuggled herself more deeply against a throw pillow with little intention of moving until necessity demanded it.

She felt more at ease now, having bared her thoughts, if only in part, to her son and felt more hopeful about her approach to their impending conversation. She laid still and warm, staring at the television without much regard to the passing of commercials and the clockwork return of the increasingly negative weather report. Slowly, Mary's eyes began to close as the heavy sleep converged on her thoughts and ultimately silenced them.

Mary lay on her bed, adorned in her favorite sheer nightgown as Paul's body sank down upon hers gently. His mouth took control of hers with the soothing of all of a kiss's intended passion. She could feel the heat of his erection against her thigh before she parted her legs for him, expressing without words what she desired most. His lips never left hers as he entered her saturated depths, the fullness of his cock expanding her inner walls to entrench itself inside her. Gently he began to take her, the thrusts of his hips deep and powerful. Mary gave in; gave herself to Paul without thought or care. Desiring only to have him stay inside her forever, she wrapped her thighs around his waist, locking her ankles behind him. She flexed her legs, tugging him into her as he pressed forward. Her groans of pleasure filled his mouth as her tongue moved past his lips in search of its mate. In that perfect moment, Mary was a lover to her son, careless of all inhibition. Lustfully, she raked her fingernails down his back until digging them into his young muscular bottom. He took her at her unspoken word and began to penetrate her harder. His lips broke from hers, gasping desperate moans of pleasure and she became aware of the pulsing swell inside her womanhood indicating that he was to fill her with his steaming warmth. She wanted to cry out to him; to tell him to climax and how much she craved the feel of his orgasm, but a strange ringing began to pull her attention away. She looked around her bedroom, frantic to find its source. It grew louder and more intrusive. Paul seemed to notice it to and pulled away from her. Mary reached out to him but his presence had left her room and the ringing only grew louder.

Mary woke with a start, wincing at the abrupt intrusion of light against her alert eyes. Her surroundings were as she had left them. The television was showing a car commercial and outside the living room window, the heavy snowfall had not ceased as the reports had promised. The only break in the normalcy of her settings was her cell phone, buzzing and ringing where she had left it on the arm of the sofa. She snatched it up, suddenly full of dread that it was Paul calling; that he had been in an accident or worse.

To a mixture of relief and annoyance, the touch screen glowed with Samantha's name as the incoming call. Mary tapped it reluctantly.

"Hey Sam." She said, still half asleep and as politely as she could, given the reluctance to abandon what she had awoken from.

"Char, great! I need a favor." Samantha replied, forgetting the social grace of a greeting of her own.

"What's up?" Mary replied, sitting up and grasping the TV remote to mute the weatherman's faithful and continuous update.

"The power over here has been flickering on and off a lot recently and I'm really concerned for all the food I have in my freezer if we lose power for good. Do you have room in that spare icebox in your basement?" Samantha enquired with an overly applied sweetness in her voice that she only wore when she needed something really badly.

"Yeah that's no problem, if you actually feel brave enough to drive over in this in your car." Mary answered.

"Normally I wouldn't be caught dead trying." Samantha replied. "I'm really not worried about the normal stuff in the fridge. That's easy enough to replace, but if all this meat I have in the freezer dies I'm out a few hundred bucks." She explained with obvious concern in her voice.

"Well send me a text then when you're on your way and I'll come out and give you a hand." Mary answered as she pulled the quilt of her body less than willingly, with the intention of getting off the couch.

"No need; the cars already packed up and I'm heading out the door now. Give me five minutes. Char, you're the best!" The line clicked dead. Mary shook her head in amusement. Of all the things she could rely upon in life, death and taxes paled in comparison to Samantha's uncanny ability to rope Mary into a plan with the assumption of her agreement. Less than willingly, she peeled her lethargic body from its entrenched place on her sofa, draped her warm quilt back over the rear of the couch and rose to her feet on sleepy legs. They carried her faithfully to her hall closet where she stepped her feet into a pair of unlaced fur lined boots and donned one of Paul's winter coats that he had left behind without bothering to pull her hair out of the collar. She caught a glimpse of herself in the foyer mirror. The jacket looked like she had stolen it from a man twice her size and it wrapped more like a thick Gortex cocoon around her body and hung around her shoulders like it was on a clothing hanger three sizes too small. Mary tucked her face into one of its lapels; it smelled like her son's musky cologne. The beast within again grumbled as it lay in her depths, dreaming and waiting to be reawakened.

Much to Mary's relief, before any further dwelling on her part occurred; her attention was redirected to the pane of glass beside her front door where up the street, a slowly moving and almost entirely snow covered red car was trudging through the deep white winter wasteland towards her house through what could no longer be recognized as a neighborhood. As she opened the front door, a blustery arctic gale struck Mary square in the face, immediately sapping away more warmth than her body could replenish. Stepping out off her front step she sank almost to her hips and began making her way through the frozen swamp that her yard had become to the street where Samantha was pulling up. Her car crunched to a halt and the engine died off as though relieved to be through an ordeal.

"I made it!" Samantha sprang from the driver's side, her hands held aloft her head triumphantly and she began to dance in the heavy snow like a victorious boxer after a grueling match. "You're a life saver Char!" She chimed, pointing at Mary like she was a savior as she rounded her vehicle in heavy high steps until she came at last to the shallow side of her trunk where the snow was worn down by the force of her car. "It's really not that much I promise!" She added as she clicked her key fob, popping the truck open to reveal four rather heavy looking brown paper bags packed to the brim with sealed freezer bags.

"It's fine Sam; I'm happy to help." Mary assured her as she labored to make her own way to the trunk where Samantha thankfully loaded both her arms with one bag each before attempting to underarm two of her own and coaxing the trunk shut with her elbow after several tries. The walk back felt treacherous as the pair tried to use the deep foot prints Mary had made on the way out. After freezing nearly to death in several failed attempts to work her front door open, she and Sam sighed in mutual appreciation for the house's warmth. Their shoes squeaked against Mary's polished hardwood foyer floor leaving wet dragging footprints as they wound around the kitchen towards the basement.

"So... How are ya holding up?" Sam asked as they descended the creaky wooden steps into the dark damp smelling lower floor. Without warning, excitement swelled out of Mary's lips.

"Paul called me not too long ago!" She chimed back, realizing that the answer sounded more elated than she would have liked. "The storm forced the ski lodge to close and he's on his way home!"

"In this?!" Samantha stammered, her voice cracking under the strain of the load of paper bags she was hauling in her weakening arms. "That's insane! It'll take him hours to get that car through the storm. He'd be better off finding a motel for the night." She grunted in relief as her feet found the steadier cool concrete floor at the base of the stairs.

"I know. I'm worried about it too." Mary admitted despite her enthusiasm. "But at least when he gets here we can talk and..." She huffed as she set her load on the floor and panted away her racing heart beat. "...we can talk and get a handle on this." She concluded with one last heavy breath before pulling open the lid of the storage cooler. Samantha plopped the remaining bags down beside Mary's set and accounted her friend cautiously.

"Char..." She began nervously, clearly uncertain as how to approach her next question. "Say the two of you talk, and you convince each other that continuing this... relationship if that's what you want to call it, isn't in either of your best interests. What then?" Mary began to pull meat from the bags and set it into the freezer quietly contemplating her friend's question. "Do you really think it will all just go back to the way it was?" Samantha probed harder as she began to empty items into the fridge as well.

"Part of me wishes it all would." Mary sighed. "I don't have to tell you what a mess this has all made of me." She added as she crushed an empty paper bag down and started in on the next one.

"But if you could rewind and go back; change things... would you?" Sam asked.

"In my right mind I would say yes, absolutely!" Mary replied flatly. "But that's the problem. Whenever I think of Paul now I know I'm not in my right mind."

"Someone else is doing the thinking huh?" Sam asked, staring down at Mary's waist with a click of her tongue. Her friend rolled her eyes at the crude remark.

"Something like that." Mary replied and then stopped her work to stand up and stare forward silently. "Or nothing like that." She added in confusion. "When I think about Paul now, yes obviously it's arousing." She tried to explain. Samantha grinned and nodded in agreement. "But the more I let it affect me the more I start to think it's something else too."

"Meaning?" Samantha huffed as she lifted a rather large piece of freeze dried meat into the freezer.

"I get... warm." Mary began as she placed her hand over her stomach. "I feel light and tingly. My heart starts pounding and..." Mary went on absentmindedly putting words to her unresolved feelings before Samantha stood and placed a hand on her arm.

"Char? Are you in love with Paul?" She asked with a tone of concern.

"What?!" Mary spat in a raised voice. "Of course not!"

"Um, it sounds to me like you are. I mean it's been a while for me and all but last I checked, that's what you feel like when you're falling in love." Samantha countered. Mary stared back at her in disbelief. The mere idea was nonsensical.

"Sam, seriously. He's my son!" Mary countered.

"Last I checked, that excuse hasn't gotten in your way a whole lot." Samantha shrugged. Mary watched in dumbfounded silence as her friend nonchalantly continued to empty meat into her freezer.

"Alright this conversation is over!" She demanded angrily. "I have no idea what I actually feel and I don't appreciate your label for it." Mary stated menacingly. Samantha backed up with her hands raised in surrender.

"Char, I'm sorry. Look I'm not trying to tell you what you feel. I call it how I see it. My aim was off, that's all." She apologized. Mary's enflamed countenance faded slightly back to its normal appearance. Samantha looked terrified and ashamed. Mary wondered if she had involuntarily come across sterner than she had intended. Her best friend looked like a child that had just realized she had crossed a line with a parent.

"No, I'm sorry." Mary dissolved into shame. "Sam, I really have no idea what I feel that's all." She tried in vain to explain. As she stood there a moment staring at her friend hopelessly, a frightening sort of sense evolved out of Samantha's accusation. Mary shrugged it off forcefully, not wishing to give the idea any more substance. "Do you want some coffee?" She finally asked, elated when Samantha nodded appreciatively, hoping that the subject was closed. The pair ascended the steps sluggishly, taking the folded paper bags back up with them.

"What's on TV?" Samantha asked tilting her head towards the living room as she followed Mary into the kitchen.

"Nothing. I was just watching the weather this morning; keeping track of the storm." Mary explained as she fished through the cupboard for a pair of clean mugs. "If you haven't got anywhere to be for a while you can always skim through the channels and find something for us to watch. That is of course if you don't mind unearthing your car later and I haven't completely scared you away yet."

"Char I'm fine. It was my fault. Anyhow I doubt there's much to watch. I was trying to find something on while I was home and I couldn't, but what the Hell. I'll see to the television; you get the coffee." Sam schemed, seeming a bit lighter in her speech now that the last embers of her friends anger were quenched. Mary simply nodded in agreement as she added creamer to her own mug while her friend turned on her heals towards the living room kicking off her heavy boots in the end of the foyer as she went.

"In love with Paul indeed..." Mary suddenly thought as the notion came flooding back into her mind. She stopped what she was doing with a heavy sigh and stared forward at the cabinet door before her as though it would answer any of the volumes of questions that were surfacing in her head. The possibility that she was even less in control of her emotions than she was of her body made her feel impossibly weak. All of Paul's life she had loved him, but with a mother's love; the love that nurtured him, protected and guided him into adulthood to the best of her ability. The notion that it was at all possible that her love for him had changed so drastically, all because of what Mary wanted to attribute to a poorly aimed sexual vulnerability, seemed utterly ridiculous. Yet as Mary tried to shrug off the sensitivity she felt inside when Paul came to mind, Samantha's accusation seemed to support more weight. She felt as hopelessly juvenile as a teenager, falling madly in love with the first boy she believed would give her his heart in exchange for her body. It wasn't a pleasant feeling at all. After finishing up both heated concoctions, she slipped her frozen feet out of her own wet boots and left them in the kitchen.

Samantha was dutifully channel surfing as Mary entered the living room with the two hot coffee mugs that would ward off the chill in their bones. She sat beside her friend and silently stared forward at the screen, oblivious to what was on it as her brain tackled what it clearly considered more important questions. Samantha grabbed Mary's trusty quilt and tossed it over the both of them before snuggling herself into a cozy place.

"Could I be in love? Is it possible? What's wrong with me?!" She thought. Her mind grappled with the questions one after the other, each seeming to lead back into the next in an endless loop of brain numbing repetition.

"Do I get one of those?" Samantha asked, breaking Mary's train of thought abruptly. She laughed and handed Samantha's coffee to her and went back to staring forward. "Are you ok Char?" Samantha asked after accounting for Mary's silence a moment.

"I was thinking about what you said in the basement." Mary confessed before giving her attention to her own cup with a shallow sip. The coffee penetrated her body richly, fighting away an approaching shiver. Samantha looked back at her with sorrow in her eyes.

"Char, I didn't mean anything bad by it." Sam recoiled, her body languge becoming defensive in preparation for more arguement.

"No I know you didn't." Mary sighed, finally making eye contact. "It's just on my mind now. What if I am?" She asked mournfully.

"What if you are... what? In love with Paul?" Samantha repeated, easing forward with caution. "Well, damn Mary I have freaking clue. Certainly would put a spin on things wouldn't it?" She answered.

"Meaning?" Mary asked as she sipped her coffee and set it back down on the table before her, discarding it as still being too hot for her tastes.

"Well I mean, before it was just sex. If you think you're in love, are you looking for some kind of relationship with him?" Samantha reasoned cautiously, obviously not wanting to enflame her friends rage again. Mary didn't take the bait and just stared forward again, trying to still the beating of her heart which had begun to build in intensity.

"No." She finally answered flatly. "No I'm not. Or yes... damn it Sam, I really have no clue what I'm thinking or what to do or..." She rambled helplessly. Samantha reached out, gingerly placing her hand on Mary's thigh.

"It's not like you have to figure all this out right now Char." She offered, setting her own mug down on the coffee table beside Mary's before addressing her further. "That's the whole point of talking to Paul when he gets home right? To straighten out your thoughts?"

"And decide where it goes from here." Mary added with closure.

"Exactly. So for now, shut up and relax. You're going to give yourself an aneurism." Sam lectured. "Let's just watch some TV and; well maybe not cause there is really nothing at all on worth watching." She grumbled as she tapped through the channels in defeat. Mary chuckled in amusement.

"Try 'on-demand'." She suggested as she rolled her head from side to side, sighing in relief as it cracked. "I really don't care so whatever you pick is fine."

"Well now. What's this?" Samantha's voice chimed merrily, breaking Mary's moment of peace. On the screen read the heading, 'recently viewed', and beneath it the words, 'Horny Moms 2'. Mary cocked her head slowly over to Samantha, regarding her amused playful look with distain.

"Paul." She answered flatly. "I'm pretty sure that's what I caught him watching that first morning."

"Scene of the crime huh?" Samantha grinned. "Well why don't we just have a little peek." She added enthusiastically as she scrolled the cursor on the screen down over the movie title.

"Oh God Sam, really?" Mary protested. "Surely there's something else on actually worth watching."

"What? It's just good fun. Besides, like I said, I was channel surfing before I called you and there really isn't anything worth watching; even you saw that!" Samantha said, discarding her friend's disapproval. "Plus..." She added after a moment's thought. "It might help you get in Paul's head a little; see what he likes... and, you could probably use something to fuel whatever happens tonight." She chimed with a playful bump of her elbow into Mary's ribs.

"Owe!" She protested again and reached out to try to snatch the remote from Sam. "Paul and I are going to talk tonight and nothing more until we do." She shot back.

"And I hardly need any help fueling my desires." She thought as she tried again to grab the remote in vain.

"Ugh-uh." Sam muttered flatly. "You said whatever I wanted to watch, and besides; 'Horny Moms 2'?" She continued to poke fun. "How can you resist?" Samantha laughed out loud. Mary simply shook her head in reply.

"Too bad..." Samantha's voice rang back. "You need to lighten up anyhow. Now, shall we pick up where Paul left off or start from the beginning?"

"Whatever..." Mary groaned, now a bit at odds with her suggestion that Samantha stick around for coffee. Nearly oblivious in her annoyance to Sam's observation that Paul had only gotten ten minutes into the porno, she rolled her eyes as her friend opted to pick up from the moment Mary had caught her son masturbating and pushed play on the remote control. The load screen scrolled its status bar only a moment before the screen lit up to exactly where Mary remembered it being before Paul had turned it off.

A mature looking but gorgeous brunette woman that Mary decided instantly was right around her age was bent over on all fours. Beneath her a younger girl, probably only in her mid twenties lay in perfect position to lather her tongue against the older porn stars vagina while a young man, near the age of the girl on the floor groaned pierced the mature beauty with a cleanly shaven and handsome looking cock. In spite of herself, Mary felt the warm rush of her blood rising to the surface of her pale skin.

"Well well well..." Samantha teased as she looked Mary over. "I do believe someone's blushing."

"Shut up." Mary groaned, rolling her eyes but they found themselves fixed back on the screen almost immediately.

"Well I can't blame you. That's fucking hot!" Sam remarked as she too looked back to the television. Mary stared at the trio intently, listening to the endless cries of pleasure the girls emitted as the younger man grunted like some silly ape above them.

"I never understood porn." Mary finally said after a few minutes. "The guys all have great bodies, but ugly faces and the women don't sound real. They just scream and moan because it's what gets guys off." She added with all the seriousness of a stern debate. Samantha turned her head and gave Mary the look one would expect had she said something naive.

"You're right, you don't get it." She stated flatly. "Char its fantasy. It's people fucking. Who cares what they say or how they sound. Next you're going to tell me the lighting is bad or the backdrop looks staged. You're paying attention to the wrong things. Look at them." She pointed to the screen. Mary looked back in time to see the two girls rolling away from the young man. Eagerly they had risen to their knees before him; their hands cupping their breasts and their tongues out like panting dogs as the man jacked extremely fake amounts of semen into their faces.

"Oh come on!" Mary complained as though she were a film critic. "Now that's just nonsense. I have never met a man who came that much. It's all fake!" She whined. Samantha shook her head quietly.

"Of course it's fake. Who cares? Char it's porn. It's hot slippery guilt free fantasy. You watch it, you get off and you're done with it!" Sam shot back, defending the movie as the scene faded to black around the two women licking the sperm off each other's faces, as though any woman had actually ever done anything so crude in real life.

"Oh yeah? I don't see you over there getting off so what's the point of this?" Mary looked at Sam out of the corner of her eye. Her friend smiled sheepishly and turned her head back to the screen as a new scene in the film came up.

"Right. Like you wouldn't completely freak out if I just dropped my pants and went to town on myself." Samantha chided.

"Even you aren't that uninhibited." Mary replied under her breath as she surveyed the screen. Another woman near her age was lying out by a pool, sunbathing topless. In the background a young man no more attractive than the last was pretending to check the waters chlorine levels. Mary rolled her eyes again, mentally predicting exactly how the scene was going to play out.

"Well I don't see you doing anything either." Samantha replied, glaring at Mary despite probably knowing how empty the argument was given Mary's initial reluctance to watch the movie at all. Mary didn't reply and just gazed forward. Samantha stared at her so hard she could feel her eyes in the corner of her peripheral vision. "Alright, fine." Samantha huffed and after leaning forward enough to set her mug on the coffee table, reached under the quilt and began to wiggle around. Mary watched Sam rummage for a moment before her jeans hit the floor at the base of the couch in a heavy flop.

"What are you doing?!" Mary demanded as the sudden motion tore her eyes from the older woman who already had the man's cock buried in her mouth.

"What does it look like?" Samantha replied as she suddenly whipped her pants out from under the quilt and tossed them carelessly on the coffee table nearly missing their drinks.

"No you aren't!" Mary shouted in amazement, her eyes fixed on her friend whose face suddenly flushed with arousal.

"Oh yes I am!" Samantha moaned as her head rocked back. "Take a good look Char. This is how you're supposed to watch a porno." She gasped as she tensed up and then relaxed with a heavy sigh of pleasure. "What's the big deal anyhow? I've got the blanket over me; it's not like you can see what I'm doing."

"What you're doing next to me!" Mary retorted in frustration. "Under my blanket. On my couch!" She added raising her voice.

"Would you calm down?!" Samantha groaned as she stared forward at the television with the glazed eyes of lust. "I've still got my panties on. Your couch is fine..." Her words dissolved into a heavy gasp of pleasure. Mary stared at her in bewilderment as the realization that Samantha had never been all that met the eyes sank in to the fullest that she could fathom.

"I can't belive you." Mary huffed and turned her head back to the screen where the woman was now squatting over the young man's hips, spearing herself down on his cock with rapid bounces. Beside her, Samantha continued to groan as she masturbated without regard to Mary's presence.

"You know you'd be a lot less uptight if you'd just join me." She moaned.

"Not gonna happen." Mary retorted as she fidgeted to her left to blatantly put distance between herself and Sam. As she wiggled over however she became aware that she had grown severely wet despite her discontent.

"Fine..." Samantha replies dismissively. "Be a prude. I'm sure Paul will love you for that." Samantha stabbed. Mary slashed her eyes across Samantha with a furious glare.

"I am not a prude!" She shouted. Samantha abandoned her self-gratification and turned her body to face Mary's fiery stare.

"Yeah? Prove it then. Take your pants off." She challenged. "This got Paul off, it's sure as Hell gonna work for me if you shut up long enough..." She stated with agitation. "You're the only one so far who isn't enjoying it so I'm calling you out. You say you're not a prude; prove it!" She demanded and then turned back towards the screen and groaned heavily as she sank her hand back into her underwear.

Mary glared at her speechlessly. On the television, the woman was laying face down over a yoga ball that had mysteriously come out of nowhere as her young lover plowed into her from behind. Mary however could only gaze in wonder at Samantha who despite the intensity of her recent argument had relaxed back into her efforts and was breathing heavily while she watched the movie and masturbated.

"You have no right to judge me." She finally whispered at her friend. Samantha rocked her head to the side to regard Mary who now was feeling more hurt than anything.

"Char, if you don't learn to let go of yourself sexually, how do you expect this thing with Paul is going to play out?" She asked with a perfectly serious tone. Mary felt stunned at the sincerity of the question. Without knowing why her hands moved of their own accord under the blanket. Samantha raised an eyebrow at her friend curiously as she offered a sly grin. Mary stared back at her as she hooked her thumbs into the waist band of her yoga pants and raised her bottom off the sofa.

"Keep going." Samantha encouraged. Mary swallowed hard and began to press the fabric down until it slid past her hips to her knees. She paused, watching Samantha's reaction which had become extremely fixated in her direction. Like a child knowing she was doing something wrong, Mary cautiously pushed the flimsy pants over her knees and let them fall to the floor at her feet before kicking them out onto the floor under the table. "Almost there..." Samantha teased, urging her to continue. Mary's heart was beating at nearly debilitating pace as she ran the palm of her hand up her thigh and hooked her fingers under the edge of her thong. The second they touched the delicate throbbing flesh of her labia, Mary shut her eyes and gasped out in pleasure. "That's my girl!" Samantha giggled as she turned back to the television to watch the woman on scene gyrate forward forcefully each time the man sank his cock into her.

Mary moved her fingers slowly over the slippery outer surfaces of her sex. She was far wetter than she had believed and her love channel opened in a delicious spasm, ready to except penetration. Her eyes darted between the television and Samantha who was herself, completely engrossed once again into pleasuring herself. The creature inside her growled for attention and as if to quench the fire it was breathing inside her loins, Mary sank her fingers deeply inside herself.

"Oh God!" She gasped as her vagina twitched and clenched down on her probing fingers. Beside her Samantha groaned heavily, as if feeding her mounting lust with Mary's. Something about her friend so aware of her vulnerability made Mary's sex ignite. Feverishly she began to rock her fingers in and out of her pussy, adding her other hand into her panties to run her fingers over her clit. Mary began to forcibly gyrate in place.

"Easy there sweetie. There's still a lot of movie left." Samantha teased as she pulled the quilt down into her lap. Mary gazed in wonder as Sam used her only free hand to lift her blouse up over her braless, milky white breasts. Her nipples were flush and hard as she seized one in her finger tips, groaning heavily as she tweaked it from side to side. In her heightened hormonal state Mary stared at them in wonder. "You can touch them if you want to." Sam cooed as she shot her friend a sideways glance of devilish playfulness. Without thinking, Mary pulled her moist fingers from her clit and reached out with a trembling hand. Samantha giggled and caught it in her own tenderly and placed it over her breast. Mary squeezed gently, instantly transported back to her early college years of bisexual experimentation. Samantha's back arched as she moaned heavily at Mary's touch. "Oh that feels nice..." She whispered as Mary rolled her friends erect nipple between her shaking fingertips.

Mary glanced back at the screen. The scene had dramatically changed. The mature lustful beauty on the television had been pulled into the pool but was leaning over the edge with her legs dangling in the water. Behind her, the young man was playfully slapping her ass with his erection. Mary felt her inner muscles contract more tightly around her fingers, which at this point had begun to move as though their actions were as involuntary as blinking. Mary reached across Sam's gorgeous chest and clasped her fingers tightly around her other breasts which mashed plumply into her palm as sweetly as the first had.

"Bet you anything he's gonna take her in the ass." Samantha suddenly commented as she stimulated herself far more obviously under the quilt. Mary stared intently at the screen to see that true to her friend's prediction, the woman had reached back behind her and was now spreading her cheeks apart in her hands as the young man positioned the head of his cock against the tight puckering entrance to her rectum. Mary's eye widened in a rich mixture of excitement and wonder as the camera closed in on the woman's ass opening up around the swollen mushroom head of the invading penis, allowing it effortless entry into her sucking anus. "That's so fucking hot!" Sam cried out as she tightly gripped the breast that Mary wasn't fondling and began to stimulate her vagina so forcefully that the quilt over her lap drifted off her slender silky legs and onto the floor leaving both friends extremely more exposed to each other. Mary stared down at Samantha's finger filled panties. They were a lacy off white and soaked through. The heavy grunts of pleasure escaping the female porn stars mouth pulled her gaze back to the screen to see the young man pounding into her; the pool water around his hips splashing loudly.

"Incredible..." Mary whispered as she watched the fullness of the man's erection vanish and reappear from his co-star's asshole in rapid deep movements. "I don't know how she does that." She added breathlessly as she pulled her hand from Samantha's breast and used it to keep her panties to one side as she fingered herself vigorously.

"What? You mean you never..." Samantha began, her own voice almost unintelligible amidst her desperate moans of pleasure.

"I tried once..." Mary stammered as the furious pleasure in her womb screamed at her for more. "... Back in high school. Didn't end well!" She gasped as she found herself once again staring back down to her side at Samantha's hand manipulating her sex under her panties. Taking notice of the attention, Samantha smiled and paused, only long enough to pull her panties completely off her legs before she spread them widely, draping one over Mary's knee before returning her fingers back to the devotion of her completely shaved vagina.

"Better?" She mused as she stared over at Mary with her lower lip in her teeth. Mary didn't answer with anything more than a deeply appreciative nod. "Good... now what were you saying?" She asked as she turned her head back to the furious anal sex that continued on the television. Mary, extremely tantalized with the silky feel of Sam's draped leg on her thigh, tugged her panties further to the side to offer reciprocation as best as she could. Samantha looked down at her friends more revealed vagina and licked her lips with a giggle.

"I have no idea..." Mary panted as she pinched her clit between her slippery fingers.

"Something about high school..." Samantha replied, her voice ripe with amusement.

"Oh..." Mary panted. "I was saying that I tried it with a boyfriend and it didn't work. He wouldn't fit and it hurt; haven't tried since." She explained. The scene on camera had changed again. The man was now lying with his legs hanging down into the pool. The woman was riding him, his cock still buried deeply into her rectum as she planted her hands on his chest to support her movements.

"You should try with Paul." Samantha moaned, pulling Mary's attention from the screen again to the gorgeous woman beside her so carelessly pleasuring herself.

"Yes let's just let my son know how much of a whore his mother has become lately." Mary thought although the damage the suggestion had done had already redirected her thoughts to shamelessly bending over and offering her anus to her son's throbbing cock.

"I'd be too afraid. He's too big." She replied instead as she attempted to redirect her thoughts from the invading fantasy by looking at the delightful mess her best friend was making between her legs. Samantha's fingers were keeping her vaginal lips spread wide as she rapidly ran her other hand over her clit in elated ecstasy. She was staring at Mary again, using her desire to feed her own as her eyes seemed to read Mary's mind.

"That's not what you're really thinking." Sam whispered. "You're thinking about his cock pressing your asshole open right now. You're thinking about how hot it would be to give that to him." She teased. Mary groaned heavily as the idea flooded her mind again. Her eyes had lost focus as she pleasured her vagina now as deeply as her fingers would permit; three of them stabbing into her sex with delightful force. She couldn't deny that the prospect of having her first successful anal sex with Paul's perfect cock; the notion of her own son being the first to really have her that way, sent the voltage coursing through her body into a brutal power surge.

"Do you trust me?" Samantha whispered as she suddenly stopped touching herself. Mary barely registered the question as she stared down at Sam's open, wet and positively delicious looking vagina.

"Yes..." She whispered back, unwilling herself to stop her self-indulgent labors. She watched intently as Samantha leaned in closer to her and drew her fingertips along Mary's inner thigh, forcing her skin to react electrically in her current state.

"Scoot down." Sam instructed, nodding her head toward the floor. Mary hesitantly obeyed, shifted her bottom towards the edge of the sofa. She watched as Samantha drew her juicy fingers into her own mouth and began to fellate them heavily. Each time she drew them out of her lips they were noticeably wetter with her saliva.

"What are you doing?" Mary asked, suddenly broken from the spell of her arousal as she watched Samantha drop her wet fingers downward.

"Trust me..." Samantha whispered, shaking her head in dismissal. "Keep doing what you're doing." She instructed. Mary continued to probe herself steadily but remained fixed on her friends hand as it moved between her legs and up under her bottom.

"Sam!" Mary gasped as she realized her friend's intent.

"Relax Char. You said you trusted me." Samantha whispered soothingly just before Mary felt the wet pressure of fingertips against her anus. Mary swallowed her gasps hard and looked over fearfully into her friends kind warm eyes. The pressure against her asshole built as Sam pushed in until the tight seal of her rectum broke, allowing a single one of Sam's fingers a slow delicious entry.

"Oh my fucking God!" She cried out as Samantha gently rocked it in and out, eased largely by the slipperiness her mouth had provided. Mary feverishly attacked her clit, spurred on by the amazing new sensation spreading through her body like a virus. Samantha continued her labors, gently probing her finger in and out of Mary slowly until she was completely relaxed around it.

"Ready for more?" Sam asked. Mary nodded hastily in reply, feeling so empowered in the moment of discovery that she felt confident enough to handle whatever her friend had in mind for her.

"Please Sam... please..." She begged. Samantha leaned in closer, resting her head on Mary's shoulder. Without thinking Mary tugged her tank top down exposing her heavy breasts. Samantha leaned lower, extending her tongue to playfully flick it across one of Mary's stiff nipples. Mary groaned at the tickling pleasure as she felt the soft sting of her anal channel spread apart for Sam's second raiding finger. A sharp sear of pain suddenly spread through her bottom at the feel of being so stretched. Mary tensed involuntarily and her friend ceased all movement.

"Its ok sweetie... just relax. I promise that will pass ok?" She asked reassuringly. Mary nodded and warily settled back into place. The moment her anal muscles eased, Samantha resumed pressing in her other finger until it rested fully extended into Mary's rectum. The sensation was incredible. Slowly and cautiously, Sam began to press her hand in and out, guiding her slender digits. Mary felt overwhelmed with desire as she closed her eyes, imagining that Paul was taking her. Her own hand resumed its rapid wanderings into her vagina. The feeling of being so full, of such completeness warped Mary's libido into explosive overdrive.

"I can't believe how good that feels!" She cried out. Samantha moaned softly as she closed her lips over her friends heaving breasts, suckling Mary sweetly. Her fingers pumped in with faster repetition, sending the hair on the back of Mary's neck outward. The pressure suddenly built in her loins like a tidal wave.

"Oh God Sam I'm gonna cum!" Mary screamed as her hips raised her upward. Samantha sank her fingers in and out faster and harder. The pleasure was too much. Mary began to shake and babble incoherently. Her own fingers fell from her vagina and wound into her friends hair, keeping her lips locked over her breast. "Sam, make me cum! Please!" She shrieked. Her friend moaned heavily against her soft flesh at the force of Mary's request. With reckless abandon she drove her fingers in and out, launching Mary over the edge.

"Oh God! Oh my fucking God!" She shrieked as she climaxed; her labia quivering as a light trickle of involuntary female ejaculate streamed from her core and out against the rug beneath her curled toes. Samantha released Mary's breast from her mouth, biting her lip in a lustful grin at the sight of the projectile orgasm. "It's too much... too much!" Mary shouted as she pushed against Sam's arm. Gently, Sam withdrew her fingers from Mary's tightest depths and wrapped her arms around her, holding her tightly as she gasped for breath. Softly, she placed her hand over Mary's trembling vagina, massaging it gently as her friend's breathe taking climax faded.

"See? It's not so bad..." Sam whispered. Mary panted for air as a droplet of sweat ran down the side of her face.

"I can't believe we did that." She replied as she shamelessly placed her own hand over Samantha's slippers fingers and helped her sooth her trembling labia. Samantha giggled.

"If we're being honest here, I've actually wanted you for years." She replied as she loosed her arm from around Mary and sat back to look into her eyes.

"You never said anything." She replied, a bit taken aback.

"You never acted like you were interested." Sam explained flatly as she wiggled her upper body to allow her blouse to fall back over her gorgeous breasts. "And I know that it was only partly me that you were thinking about just now, but I'll take what I can get. Besides, learning a little about anal play really can't hurt your situation." She added as she reached out to the table in search of her moist underwear.

"Not sure I follow, but I'm not complaining." Mary admitted curiously.

"Well..." Sam replied as she stepped her lovely legs into her panties and scooted them back up over her hips. "When you told me about you can Paul, I didn't hear anything about a condom. So unless you're on the pill..." She paused reaching for her pants.

"I'm not." Mary admitted shamefully. "I have condoms; we just... I completely forgot to..."

"Exactly. So unless you two are just fine and dandy with having a child of your very own..." Samantha continued with a tone of caution. Mary visibly shuddered at the terrifying notion. "Yeah I didn't think so." Samantha declared taking account of her friend's reaction. "Well, now you have another option until you get safe or one of you can actually remember to wrap him up." She concluded, sitting back on the sofa, staring at Mary who still found it difficult to summon the will to move for her own clothes.

"I don't think you can really compare Paul to a couple of fingers." Mary answered in reservation as the gorgeous memory of her son's ample size filled her mind in apprehension.

"Maybe not at first..." Sam interrupted. "But I assure you it's all the same in the end if you're gentle and go slow. It can be just another completely intimate experience for you two." She chimed happily.

"What about this? I mean you and me?" Mary asked, suddenly remembering Sam's earlier confession. Despite her desire for her son, she could not but be aware of the strong new connection that she and Sam had just made in their friendship.

"Really Char, let's be honest with each other." Samantha grinned. "All fun aside, you are devoted to Paul even if you haven't figured that out yet. I was just in the right place at the right time. I'm not complaining but I'm nothing compared to what's going on there." She added as she leaned up to look out the living room window. "I had better get going before I can't find my car." She sighed. Mary's heart leapt into her throat. Her friend had all the seeming of a rejected third date.

"Sam..." Mary whispered. "You never said anything to me..." She began despite another of her friends dismissive waves to stop her short. "I feel awful now." She confessed. "You don't need to just rush off." She added, placing a hand on her friends in earnest caring.

"Char you are my best friend. You were before I got here and you will be when I leave and I will always be there for you." Samantha said warmly with her brilliant smile. "As far as rushing off goes; I'm not. I just really don't want to be snowed in here and if I'm around when Paul comes home..."

"He and I can always talk some other time." Mary interrupted.

"No. You need to talk now. You need to decide what this means to you two and you need to do it before both of you worry yourselves to death. He may have sounded calmer than you on the phone but he's an eighteen year old boy and is probably struggling with this more than you. You at least have me to talk to. I bet he wouldn't dare tell a single one of his friends what happened." Samantha reasoned. Until that moment, Mary had not considered the idea and began to focus her thoughts more on her son, lost in all of this as she was with no outlet. "See? You know that I'm right." Sam said as she stood up and grabbed for her pants from the floor.

"Do you know how much I love you for being here for me in all this?" Mary asked as she watched her friend slide her legs into her jeans and rock them over her butt. Sam eyed Mary playfully and leaned down to where she was sitting, still half naked and exposed. Her lips collided with hers briefly in a soft but meaningful kiss before breaking away again. Something about the simple gesture let Mary know that her friend felt anything but taken for granted and it eased her turmoil enough to smile again.

"Babe, you've always been there for me." Sam replied before sinking her feet back into her shoes and walking out through the living room. Mary watched her go until she vanished into the foyer. "I want details!" Sam shouted through the hall before Mary heard the front door open and close again. Sitting dumbfounded with her senses dulling out of hyperactivity, Mary glanced up at the television. The screen was still and blue with a highlighted message asking her if she wanted to watch the movie again. She stood up instead, ignoring the television as she settled her thong back into place and struggled to keep her balance as she stepped back into her thin black pants.

"What the hell just happened?" She remarked to herself out loud. To the best she could recall her friend had not shared in climax with her and the hurried manner about her departure still came across as bizarre, but the recollection of the last hour of her life could not but leave a wide smile on her face. With some newfound rejuvenation, she felt invigorated and marched back upstairs to her bedroom where the pile of mangled linen on her bed still awaited her. The next several hours blurred in a series of domesticated chores. Mary made her bed with fresh sheets and set the soiled ones in the wash. As she moved from one room to the other, she cleaned and freshened up her home, driven by an exciting happiness that she couldn't define. Outside her windows, the pale cloud covered sun had begun to set, turning the sky into a brilliant winter red. Mary made herself a modest dinner and then turned off the dining room light, allowing the sky's brilliance to light the setting of her meal through the sliding glass door to her rear patio deck.

As she placed her plate in her sink, Mary finally became aware of the time with the bright assistance of her oven's digital clock, grounding her senseless happiness back into tormented anticipation. At nine o'clock, Mary had failed to hear from Paul.

"Either he's trying to concentrate on the road or something has happened." She thought to herself; her pulse quickening in a slight moment of brief panic. Taking a long deep breath, Mary shut her eyes and composed herself, deciding that her own anticipation of his arrival was getting the best of her and that surely she would hear the front door open any time in the coming minutes. She finished her dishes and made her way back upstairs, shedding her clothes as she advanced toward the bathroom. The moment she twisted the shower knob, the piping hot water steamed the mirror in the room over and formed a heavy layer of condensation along the tile wall. Upon stepping into the stream, her skin flushed with warmth as her pours opened to allow the shower to wash the day away from her body. Her lavender bath wash filled the room with its floral scent and rejuvenated her flesh that still tingled from the afternoons frivolities. She remained in the hot downpour well after necessity required, still and calm and contemplating how best to begin her conversation with Paul. Would he begin with his thoughts, or would she have to take the lead. What would he say? Where would his thoughts be coming from; his heart or the same primal place that was plaguing her? In retaliation to any question Mary could think of regarding her son's train of thought, she realized that she had its equal opposite circulating around in her own mind. Then all at once a solid and undeniable truth fought it's way to the forefront of her brain like a blinking neon sign.

"I don't want it to stop." She whispered out loud, the water from the shower shaking off her lips. Whether it was because she could admit it to herself, or because she hadn't ever imagined that her guilt would subside to make such a declaration she couldn't be sure; but in that moment of levity a kind of acceptance towards herself erupted into Mary's consciousness. She smiled broadly as a thought about her son's body against hers came and went through her mind with almost no shame. "I don't want it to stop." She said again, grinning broadly as though the statement only felt better the more she repeated it.

"But does he feel the same way? Can he accept what kind of life this will be for both of us? What kind of life would that be?" She thought. Her happiness endured but became tempered with the wisdom that there was still much to discuss. Mary turned off the shower and stepped out onto her plush bathmat. Wrapping a towel around her dripping body, she stepped before her bathroom mirror and brushed the moisture away to see her reflection staring back. Something had changed; the figure looking back at her seemed more familiar. Mary grinned again and began to run a brush through her hair.

"Mom?!" A sudden voice called from the base floor of Mary's house causing her to drop her hairbrush in the sink with excited alarm. Without thought her legs pulled her from the bathroom, racing her down her hallway and bounding down the stairs so clumsily she had to press her hand over the tuck of her towel to keep it from whipping off behind her as she moved. Rounding the last corner and into her foyer she saw him; tired certainly, but young and beautiful and very much home. She stopped in her tracks to look at him, fearing that her legs would wobble apart if she tried to take another step. He stared back at her a moment and then began to walk forward silently.

"I'm so glad you're home." Mary sighed under her breath as she watched him advance on her yet still he remained quite silent. As the distance between them closed, Mary became aware of an energy between them that felt more focused and powerful with each of her son's slow steps toward her. Finally he was standing before her, close enough to feel the chill off of his clothes. He was staring down at her with intent and meaningful eyes. His hands reached out, gently loosening the folds of her robe, sending her heart beat into a frenzy. Mary nearly blacked out as his mouth suddenly impacted against hers and as her eyes slammed shut and as she heard the powerful need in the moan transferring from her mouth into his, she felt the towel drop off her body all together. She reached out, pulling him against her nudity, uncaring about the biting cold of his clothing as she let the world around her fall away and scrambled desperately to loosen his belt from around his waist. The moisture in her loins flowed forth as her hand reached into his pants to take hold of his rigid cock. His lips broke from hers.

"Talk later?" He whispered to her.

"Much later." She replied.

CHAPTER 4

Mary's back collided with the wall in her foyer with a forceful impact that beat the breath from her lungs as she tried desperately to keep her lips against her son's. His hands had taken hold of her wrists, pinning them against the wall beside her shoulders as his mouth devoured hers. The stinging cold of his jacket bit at her nipples, coaxing them to the blissful hardness that wrought sensitivity through her flushed moist breasts like a current. Finally her son's lips separated from hers as he rocked his head to the side of her neck. Mary gasped as she felt his teeth clench into her skin as a starving animal might having taken her for its kill. Wresting one wrist free, she raked her fingers through his hair pulling his head in tighter and inviting him to take of her body what his glorious mouth could.

"Paul!" Mary groaned as her son kissed and bit her neck. No longer giving any consideration to the unfriendly cold on her nude damp flesh, she raised her leg, hooking it around his freezing hip as she began to grind her core against his body involuntarily. The lump in his pants was so apparent Mary wondered how the seemingly thin material was able to contain his blessed cock from tearing free and impaling her as though it had its own will. His other hand released her remaining wrist at last, allowing both of his hands to streak down the sides of her body and cup her ass firmly. The leg she was trying to support herself upon was thankful for the levity of his assistance. His mouth parted from her tingling neck. Paul's eyes were alight with some desperate and carnal flame as he stared at her. The look was enough to melt Mary into complete depravity. Her hands sank between their bodies to manipulate the clasp of his belt with all the remaining ability her trembling hands could muster. Paul inched back enough to allow it as he brought one of his hands around from her tightly gripped rear and plunged between her quivering legs. The touch against her naked flowing sex brought Mary so close to climax that she had to fight to focus on the task of tugging her son's pants down from his toned hips. As the elastic of his underwear sank past his manhood his beautiful cock sprang upward, swollen and red and demanding her appreciation. As Paul's flat fingers rocked back and forth across her aching labia, Mary clasped her hand around his cock and began to tug furiously.

"Bed!" Mary gasped, barely able to get the word out as her senses relished the feel of Paul's pulsing cock wrapped so tightly in her slender fingers. The slippery lubrication of his manhood was leaking from him copiously and had begun to glisten along the marvelous length of his cock as his mother pulled and twisted her hand up and down along it. "God, Paul! Take me to bed right now!" She pleaded, tugging her son's manhood faster and faster until his eyes began to flutter in their sockets as he ripped his jacket off his shoulders and discarded it with a flick of his arm.

"That's too fucking far!" He groaned in pleasure as he kicked his boots and his pants the rest of the way off and began to peel his sweater up over his muscled chest until finally he was as properly exposed as she was. His skin, unlike the chilled garments that had clothed it was radiant of warmth as though it was conveying of its own accord its desire for her. Mary released his shaft, feeling as she did the sticky string of his pre-cum that came with her hand like a delicious tether to his cock head. Leaping at once up in the air, Paul caught her as she wrapped her legs tightly around him and dug her fingernails into the tight muscles of his back.

"Take me anywhere then!" Mary cried out as she settled down against the length of his throbbing cock between her legs against that narrow tender spot between her burning holes. "Take me anywhere!" She repeated as suckled his earlobe into her wanton mouth. "Just take me!"

Paul began to walk down the hallway past the foyer. Mary's eyes clenched shut as she kissed and suckled any inch of her son's skin her lips could taste. She didn't know where he was going; she didn't care. She ground her saturated sex down against the length of his cock, gyrating against it as she felt him walk a few more steps and then turn from the hallway. Her lips captured his earlobe again.

"I need you..." She whispered through the lewd sucking against his ear. "God Paul I need you..." Her words sounded painfully and childishly desperate even in her own ears. She prayed that it didn't sound that way to her son who now as she allowed the tightly closed lids of her eyes to open some had walked them into the kitchen and was approaching the large center island in the middle. Mary reluctantly admitted to herself that the location wouldn't have been her first choice but now as she turned her head around to see where her son was going, the cool stone covered cooking station was as welcome as any other location she could think of so long as the outcome was the same. As Paul came to a halt before it, his grip slackened and Mary slid down his body until her toes met the cool hardwood floor, feeling the shaft of his ridged cock slip the full length between her legs and jerk upward as their bodies separated, whipping along her clit as it rose back to its natural proud upward posture. The sensation was almost enough to deny her legs the ability to support her. Before she could guess as to Paul's intentions his hands clasped her waist tightly and whirled her around until she was facing the island away from him.

"Oh God I'm so ready for you, Paul!" Mary gasped as her son's strong hands pressed her upper body harshly over the edge of the cold edge of her marble kitchen counter, leaving her bottom angled back towards him longingly and knowing that the heavy saturation between her legs would help her body accommodate his ample size without effort. His fingertips dug into her bottom, parting her cheeks until she was open to his needs. Simply feeling the desperation in Paul's hands to expose her made Mary consciously aware of the moisture accumulating between her labia, which flooded over the surface as her son held her apart. Mary shut her eyes as she raised one of her toned shapely legs up and brought it alongside her upper body against the counter, preparing herself to feel the delicious impalement of her own son's magnificence. The sudden and unexpected heavy wash of her son's tongue against her vagina however forced her eyes open in blissful surprise as she realized that Paul had sunk down behind her and was in fact now burying his face in her sex from behind.

"Paul! Oh my God" She cried out as his mouth danced against her dripping opening. "Baby what are you doing? I need you inside me now!" She begged, delighted in the sensation but still almost disappointed that she wasn't already feeling the head of his cock battering against her cervix.

"I've wanted this for days." Paul grumbled behind her, barely abandoning his efforts to press his tongue inside her as he spoke. "You taste so good Mom." He mumbled again. "... So good" He repeated as he lapped at her channels trembling opening the way he had once devoured a treat when he was young. "I haven't been able to forget how amazing you taste since the last time! Oh God, Mom..." He added between passes in and out of her with his tongue. Mary's body trembled in reaction to the words. Aside from the obvious arousal to his generous compliment, she couldn't help but still become horribly hot at being identified as his mother when Paul pleasured her. Mary's eyes clenched shut as she felt her swollen labia collected together in her son's sucking lips as Paul suckled her juices from them before popping her love petals free of his mouth. Mary began to lose control of herself, writhing against the cool countertop as her son suckled her clitoris into his firmly holding lips and released it with a similarly lewd wet pop of his mouth.

"Oh fuck! Baby, that feels so good." Mary panted, growing increasingly desperate for more. Paul's hands gripped her bottom tightly, holding her cheeks apart to grant him better depth to plunge his tongue inside her sex, fucking it in and out of her like a small wet cock in his mouth. Her knuckles went white, gripping the edge of the counter as she wiggled her bottom up and down in time with the heavy passed of his tongue.

"How the hell does he know how to do this so well?" She wondered, as it began to occur to her that her son's sexual prowess possessed a lack of limitation that she never would have associated with a man his age.

"Oh fuck!" In earnest provocation, Mary cried out sharply as she felt the tight clench of Paul's teeth searing into her clit. The burning sting was as unexpected to her as how amazing it felt. Her most delicate place was at the mercy of his grinding teeth, stinging her to the core. As soon as it became too painful however, she felt him set her love button lose and the playful wash of his tongue soothed the bite way. "Oh god baby..." Mary gasped. "Bite it again." She begged. At once the sting returned this time accompanied by a tug as her son pulled her clit out with his teeth. The pain came more quickly and with greater intensity. Mary felt almost certain that her countertop would soon have finger marks in its edges from the iron clench she was imposing upon it. With a sigh of relief, she felt her clit released and again the heavy lather of his wet mouth soothed the pain away.

"Are you ok?" Paul whispered from behind her with concern, but his tone seemed more to convey a question as to whether she wanted him to do it again.

"I loved it." Mary replied in a labored whisper, continuing to rock her bottom up and down to lather her wetness against Paul's face. With eagerness he pressed his mouth back in, suckling her still stinging clit into his mouth till it met his flickering tongue. His hands tightened against her bottom, keeping her open to him as the pressure he exerted against her delicate flesh intensified and sped up dramatically. "Oh Paul don't stop!" Mary screamed as she felt the tidal wave inside her loins building towards its crest. "Lick my pussy Paul! Lick your mother's pussy! It's so fucking good!" Mary babbled as the slew of obscenities flowed from her mouth like an actress in one of her son's porno's and empowered her to let herself go. Never before had she felt so confident as to speak so freely of what she wanted with a lover; what she craved. Her usual reserved vocabulary gave way as the beast in her womb spoke with her voice. She was becoming the animal inside her and the animal had no time for proper words befitting a mother's speech. Throwing her head back, she stared up at the ceiling that spun in circles before her dazed eyes as the mouth of her flesh and blood nibbled and sucked and washed her sinful wetness clean. Her hands ached to maintain their hold on the islands edges as the one leg she kept draped up alongside her body thrashed spastically with each jerking pulse of pleasure that Paul delivered into her body.

"I'm going to cum!" She cried out as she felt the hot flood inside her crest to the magical point of climax. "God, Paul make me cum!" She pleaded. His groans of approval down behind her sounded vicious and something other than simply human. Perhaps, she thought, there was an animal inside him as well. "Oh God!" Mary screamed as she felt her vagina's walls reverberate, delivering her orgasm across her son's face in a flood of appreciation. His face still buried tightly between her toned buttocks, Paul sucked and licked frantically as though she had saved him from some cruel death from dehydration until at last he came up for air.

"Mom..." He panted catching his breath. "Incredible..." Was all he could add as Mary looked back over her shoulder at the incredible sight of her son's face bathed in her love oils. He sat on the floor panting, his body supported against his arms behind him and his cock extended between his legs, calling to her perversely. Mary grinned at the lovely sight and lowered herself off the edge of the kitchen counter, slumping to floor in front of him. She leaned back against the islands base and stared helplessly at her son's erection. With every heavy breath he took his manhood jerked with his heartbeat. Mary grinned again and extended her finger, curling it to beckon him to come to her.

"I want that." She whispered, licking her lips.

"God woman you are indeed lost." She thought to herself as she watched intently as Paul clamored to his feet and walked towards her. He stepped delicately around her legs until finally his cock was twitching inches from her mouth. Mary moaned softly at the amazing sight of the pre-cum soaked head glistening before her and opened her mouth slowly. Paul inched in until the salty taste of his juice hit the tip of his mother's tongue. Placing his hands on the edge of the counter to support himself, he pressed in farther. Mary's eyes widened as she parted her jaw wider, allowing the monstrous phallus to invade her mouth. She stared up at him; his face was pure awe.

"That looks amazing." He whispered as he rocked his hips slowly back and forth, delivering unto his mother his length inch by unbelievable inch. Mary finally reached up, taking his shaft in her hands as she slipped it from her lips with a wet kiss around the crest of the head. Gingerly, she rocked his length back and forth in her grasp.

"I love you Paul." Mary whispered. He smiled down at her. His face was warm and expressive. Leaning in, she took him back into her mouth, owning the action more than before as she let him be still as she took control. Flattening her tongue in her mouth she bobbed back and forth, letting his skin tantalize her taste buds as it had the first time she had tasted it. Her hands jerked him, coaxing his sticky fluid to spill into her mouth. She reached out, cradling the incredible set of testicles her son owned in her fingernails. His cock jumped in her mouth. Mary groaned as she felt him swell her lips apart. She leaned in deeper, until at last the thick mushroom of his cock head eased into her throat where she knew he needed it. Her eyes watered. It was difficult to maintain but in that moment she cared nothing but for her son's aching desperate pleasure.

"Mom that feels so good!" Paul gasped. Mary stared up at his face, watching his eyes clench shut. His mouth gaped with his labored breaths. Finally she pulled back, couching slightly as her throat returned to its normal shape. Paul pulled back, allowing her to recuperate. As his cock pulled from her lips, a heavy wet string of her saliva pulled with it, dripping down her chin and across her breasts. A few deep breaths was all she needed before she leaned in again, taking him back in and sucking tightly as she grazed her fingernails along the length that she couldn't consume. Again the magnificent twitch of his cock's approval jerked inside her mouth. Mary moaned passionately, rocking her head back and forth, allowing her lips to become her vagina; tight and fleshy and perfectly soft.

"Oh my God! Oh my... God!" Paul gasped under the influence of his mother's expert fellatio. Mary sucked harder as she wrapped her hand tightly around the base of his cock, jerking it forcefully as she devoured him. Her eyes never left his face, watching every clue to his pleasure now matter how subtle. "I'm going to cum! I'll cum if you want me to!" He pleaded. Mary tilted her head up and down desperately with him still locked in her mouth, moaning furiously to reply. "Oh God just... just don't stop!" Paul cried out as she sucked him with all the lust her body and mind possessed.

"Never baby... I'll never stop... God, cum for me!" Mary thought as she jerked him harder. He swelled suddenly. Mary withdrew, pumping him in her hands as she opened her mouth as wide as possible in time for the first incredibly delicious white rope of his semen to hit her full in the face.

"Oh Mom!" Paul shouted as Mary struggled to aim his climax for her outstretched tongue. She moaned thankfully as it filled her mouth with several harsh streams of released pressure. She gulped and swallowed, trying to waste as little as possible despite the amount that spilled past her lips and dripped down between her heaving breasts.

"That's it lover!" Mary cried. "Oh Paul give it all to me!" She begged, still jacking him off furiously. "My beautiful boy." She marveled as the last dripped from his purple head and splashed down along her toned abs, dribbling across her skin between her open legs.

Letting him go at last, Mary collected his semen from her body with her fingertips and sank them into her mouth. She looked up at him. His face was flush as though he had run miles to be with her, but the fire in his eyes was no less alight than before. Deep inside her loins, Mary's beast growled with renewed need.

"Take me to bed." She gasped through the rampant pulsing of her heart beat. "Please Paul, I can't wait any longer to feel you inside me!" She added as she struggled to her feet and took hold of her son's hand, dragging him along behind her. Paul trotted along behind her as she led him down into the living room and around the corner to the stairwell. The narrow ascending corridor was blurry as her beating heart pumped adrenaline into her eyes. Half way up she felt her son halt behind her, his hand ripping free of her grip.

"Come here." Paul commanded, grabbing her hips and pulling her down to her hands and knees on the steps. Mary's eyes bulged wide she felt her depths invaded by her son's massive cock. Without the slightest of effort, it seemed to push into her until she felt his hips collide with her ass and the tip of his cock ground into her as deeply as her body would allow. No sooner than she could relish in being so completely full, she felt Paul rear back and slam in again.

"Oh God, Paul yes!" Mary shouted, using the step her hands were against to push back against his hard thrusts. "Take me! Fuck me!" She wailed. Paul's fingers clenched into her waist as he tugged her body back into each stab that his beautiful cock could offered her. Her heavy breasts rocked back and forth, smacking against the step below her hands as he took her harshly. His hips spanked her with each fierce penetration sinking deeper into her womb than the last.

"Mom! Oh God, Mom!" Paul panted as he strained his burning young muscles to drive his body onward.

"Tell me you love this! Tell me you won't stop!" Mary pleaded, knowing how awful her plea sounded and sinking deeper into the joy such depravity brought with it. With each hammering sensation into her vagina, she strained as her body jolted forward; her knees grinding against carpet, lodged in the crease between steps until they stung with rug burn. "Harder!" Mary screamed, desperate to be violated. "Take me! Fuck me and never stop!" She continued to wail. Paul released her hip and Mary felt his hand travel up her arched back until it sank into her tangled hair. With a swift tug her head was wrenched back as her son rode her from behind using her hair as his reigns.

"You feel so fucking good!" Paul panted. "Mom..."

"That's it lover!" Mary panted in pleasure as ceiling she was forced to look at above her warped in her dazed vision. "Take me!" Her rear ached with the slapping of her son's toned skin as he pounded into her for all he was worth. Each time Paul lunged forward into her aching sex, the steps beneath them creaked the sounds of aged wood muffled under carpet, buckling under the pressure exerted upon them. Mary reached out, taking hold of the rails to either side of her. Locking her arms she relied on her fit core muscles to propel her body back, matching her son's stabs with the force of her own body in reverse. Each time the head of his unbelievably hard cock impacted inside her, her eyes seemed to swell with adrenalin.

"I can't take much more!" Paul whimpered breathlessly. Mary looked back over her shoulder. Her son's lovely face was bathed in perspiration and his eyes were a squinted match for his gaping mouth. Inside her she could feel his thickness widening.

"Oh god I feel that!" Mary screamed out as she tried desperately to propel herself harder back into Paul's cock. "Fill me Paul!" She pleaded as her heart beat inside her chest so hard she could not but help let go of one railing to place her hand on her heaving chest between her breasts. Paul tugged at her hips and drove her forward with impossible speed. Amidst the intensity of her pleasure, Mary could feel the tormented skin of her knees grinding painfully against the rug. "Please baby cum inside me now!" She cried out, unsure of how much more her body could endure before it gave out. Answering her prayer for his release, Paul's hands tightened along her body as his penis jerked inside her. She knew she could hear him cry out; grateful words of pleasure escaping his lips, but all she could focus on was the feel of warmth spitting into her as her lover ejaculated and coated the inside of her womb with his seed.

Mary let the railing go and slumped against the stairs. Paul at last released his tight grip upon her allowing her to relax her wobbly legs. As she did, the seal of her blissfully fucked vagina gave, allowing his gift to seep past his cock and dribble out along the length of her thighs.

"God can anything feel more perfect?" She wondered. She crawled forward up a step, groaning heavily as the length of his manhood evacuated her body until at last the head slipped past her swollen battered lips. More of his semen bubbled from her gaping core, some running down her legs, the rest dripping onto the step between her chaffed and raw knees. She lay there awkwardly on the incline, panting wordlessly until she felt her son's hands upon her skin again. His fingertips traced up and down the muscles of her back which under his touch she realized were slick with sweat. His body slumped gently down upon hers and soon she felt the hot breath of his mouth along her neck.

"Please tell me we're not finished yet..." He whispered into her ear as he kissed the salt from her flesh.

"How do you still have energy?" Mary laughed, admitting to herself that with anyone else she probably would have been long since spent. However there, with the knowledge that her son's naked body was against hers, she could not help but realize that she too was far from satiated. She rolled over under him, draping her legs aside his body. His cock was twitching with his pulse and dangerously close to her vagina once again. He leaned in, not to take her but to consume her lips with his. His kiss tasted sweet and Mary whimpered as she opened her mouth so that her tongue could dance slowly against his. He leaned in closer until Mary jumped involuntarily at the feel of his cock touching her vagina once again.

"No." She gasped breathlessly. "Bed." She added, sitting up and backing her body up the steps and out from under him. Paul smiled and stood up as she turned onto her hands and knees and raised herself up with use of the railing to her own feet and began to wobble towards her original destination. As she crossed the last step and into the hallway upstairs, Mary looked down at her knees. One was pink and chaffed. The other had in fact broken skin against the rub burn and was threatening to bleed should anything touch it. She smiled in satisfaction as though they were some perverse war wounds as she teetered towards her bedroom.

Within the room at last, her bed welcomed her eyes like a queenly throne for their lovemaking. It looked inviting and soft; something her aching body more than needed. More than that however, it was not longer her bed; it was theirs as though it always had been, their bed; their throne. Mary turned around feasting her eyes upon her son's outstanding naked form. His hair was a tangled mess, sparkling with sweat. The cut lines of his chest and abs flexed with his still heavy breaths. Her eyes lowered taking him all in. Between the rippled tone of his hips and thighs, his cock stood erect, wet and glistening with both of their orgasms. He was without a doubt the most incredible looking lover that she had ever had. Mary bit her lip as she looked back up until her wanton eyes met his lustful stare. He too seemed to be appraising her body as she had his and too her delight, his look was one of equal appreciation and longing.

"What do you see when you look at me now, Paul?" She asked.

"Someone I'm amazed I couldn't see before." He replied after a moment's consideration. "I see my mother; the most beautiful..." He began but stopped short as though his words had failed him. "I don't think I can describe who I see when I look at you anymore mom." He resigned. Mary wondered a moment if that was good or bad. "I want you more than anything I've ever wanted." He offered as he stepped closer. "I want to make you feel like you've never felt." He added, continuing to advance upon her. He was now looming over her as though he was ready to pounce. Mary swallowed harder, once again under the spell of her son's and her own lust. She loved feeling helpless against his need. She felt certain all he now had to do was look upon her in a certain way and she would instantly succumb to him no matter the time or place.

She reached out and took Paul's hand, pulling him forcefully around her toward their bed. He allowed it, going with her modest strength as compared to his and flopped down on his back. Mary crawled up over him, draping her legs over his hips and settling into a straddle until she felt the length of her son's cock between her parted swollen labia. Placing her hands on his chest she began to rock her body back and forth, sliding his shaft across her clit. Her vagina screamed at her with a burning pulse to be entered again; to be filled. Never the less, Mary playfully savored the anticipation, working her aching sex along Paul's thick phallus like she was painting its length with her juices. Only until she felt certain she would explode, did she reach between their bodies and guide him up into her vagina and settle her weight completely down.

"Oh fuck!" Paul groaned in pleasure.

"You just lay there." Mary instructed, taking her hands from his chest and raising her torso upright. Slowly, she began to rock back and forth, keeping him completely inside her; grinding the head of his cock into her womb as deeply as it would penetrate. "Oh Paul..." She moaned heavily. "That's so deep! My God baby, you're so fucking big!" She babbled torridly. It felt easy to be vocal; to express every nuance of her pleasure to her young lover. Mary let her words drip from her tongue like honey, hoping that her vulgar speech would only serve her son's pleasure as much as her own. She stared down at him with glazed bedroom eyes, biting her pouty lower lip. She held her rhythm fluid and slow, grunting as she felt the head of his cock shift around against her cervix.

Paul sat up abruptly, relaxing his weight on his hands behind him. His head tilted down, closing towards his mothers swaying chest. Mary slid her hands slowly up her stomach, cupping her breasts in her hands and offering them forward towards her son's opening mouth. His lips locked against the sensitive firm flesh of her nipple, causing her to gyrate against him harder.

"Oh my baby boy." She groaned. Paul's hands gripped tightly against his mother's, kneading her ample flesh together as his mouth dragged hot and slowly from breast to breast. He suckled her as wantonly as he had as a baby, desperate and starving for her nourishment. Now however his lips and teeth teased her for her pleasure and his own satiation to devour her milky soft skin. Mary clenched her muscles down against Paul's cock, rocking against him harder. Her loins began to reverberate as the flush of impending orgasm began to pulse though her body.

"You're close again; I can feel it. I love it when you squeeze like that." Paul panted. Mary widened her straddle, feeling him press up inside her only that much more.

"It happens so easily with you." She whispered, rocking her head back as she rode him. She pressed her left breast back into his mouth, kneading the other in her hand. "That one's more sensitive." She groaned as she felt his teeth sink into her hand nipple. "Oh Paul, that's it!" She cried out sharply as the sting drove her hips to rock harder against her son. "... So sensitive." She groaned as she released her breasts and wove her fingers into the hair behind his head, keeping his incredible mouth against her delicate breast. Paul sat up completely, keeping his head tilted to her chest but pulling her legs around until they locked behind him. His hands grabbed eagerly at her bottom, helping her grind down on his shaft which at the new angle seemed to fill into her belly.

"Paul I'm going to cum so hard for you!" She wailed in reply as she writhed against her son with invigorated force. "Just a little more..." Her voice trailed off raggedly. Her inner thighs were raw and screaming from their overworked muscles and the soft skin chaffed against her son's hips, however she was too lost in her lust to notice let alone care. Paul's hands gripped her hips firmly, pulling and pushing her pelvis back and forth; aiding her tireless body in rocking Mary to her impending release.

"Cum Mom!" Paul begged. "Please cum!"

"Just... a little... a little more... Oh fuck!" Mary screamed as the dam inside her broke. "Oh God! Paul! I'm cumming!" Her voice broke in a shrill cry as she felt her vagina release its milky nectar against her son. Breathless to the pulse of her eruption, she flattened against his chest, draping her head down alongside his. As the spasm forced her legs to unlock from around him, Paul leaned back, pulling her down on top of him. She felt his legs rise behind her bottom and at once the tremendous force of the upward stabs of his cock began to slam inside her.

"Fuck!" Mary cried out, overpowered by the sensations amplifying her climax. "Fuck Paul, it's too much!" She screamed, scrambling to try to crawl off him, finally allowing her body to admit it had reached the threshold of pleasure it would tolerate. His arms wrapped around her body tightly, holding her against his chest. She was helpless; trapped to the mercy of his passionate whims. Harder and harder she felt him pierce up into her sex with harsh slaps of his thighs against her bottom. "Oh God Paul I can't take it!" She pleaded, desperate to rest and allow the terrible pleasure he was inflicting upon her to ease, if only for a moment.

"I'll stop when you mean it!" Her son grunted in her ear as he continued to deliver relentless penetration into her core. Mary's eyes slammed shut as she fought to endure the climax that Paul seemed intent to make unending. Her screams had lost the breath it took to sustain them and she dug her teeth into his shoulder, wound her fingers into his hair and clung to him for what felt like dear life. The world around her had become a haze of vertigo and maddening intensity and she felt as a monk might, meditating his way onto a plane of existence that he had never before imagined. The only sound that permeated the disorienting state of bliss was the heavy smack of his flesh against hers.

"So much. Too much! Can't take it!" Mary babbled, having been forced well beyond the capacity to formulate complete sentences.

"Then tell me to stop." Paul whispered back. "Make me believe it."

"I can't!" She whimpered hopelessly. Her heart felt close to arrest, pulsing adrenaline through her veins as she endured the persistent coursing of ecstasy caused by the hammering cock inside her. "Paul! Oh Paul I think... I think..." She tried to convey her state but it was hopeless as a renewed rush began to flow through her vagina. Her vision went red as she felt her womanhood gush.

"Again! Again! I'm cumming... Oh God!" She screamed as her lung burned to deliver the words past her lips. Through the delirium of her thoughts she scarcely heard her son's violent groan of release and the thick swell inside her that preceded the thick wet warmth filling her body once again. Even still however, Paul made no effort to cease his assiduous assault into her aching vagina. Desperately she fought against her son's iron arms, wiggling her way free with labored effort as she gasped for air. "Enough! Enough! Stop; please I can't take more!" She beseeched him, sinking her hands between their chests and holding them against her breast as if to quell the beating of her heart and the stinging surge of the most formidable orgasm she had ever endured. Paul's arms relaxed from their unbreakable hold around his mother's shuddering body and soothed up and down her spine, caressing her skin gently and resigning to her craving for a period of stillness.

Mary lay pressed against Paul's chest, listening to the heavy pattern of his heart beating frantically within for several moments. It seemed to pound as forcefully as her own though to look at her son, she would never have guessed it. Her lungs began to take in air again with ease and she found a tiny reserve of energy to roll to the side. As she freed herself from his warmth, she groaned at the sensation of his slippery cock pulling out of her vagina, followed by the wet flood of his semen seeping out after it. She crawled with effort to position herself alongside his sculpted glistening body and sat up beside him, still attempting to catch her breath as she rocked her head to one side, resting it on his shoulder.

"That was..." Mary began, panting each word with its own breath.

"Fucking... amazing!" Paul completed her thought as he stared forward with a static gaze that might have made any onlooker think he was entranced.

"Times like this I wish I never gave up smoking." Mary panted, half jokingly as her eyes settled on the magnificent mess that both of their climaxes had deposited along his still pulsing and rigid flesh. Paul's look of curiosity burrowed into her, forcing her attention away from his penis and up into his eyes. She realized in that moment that she had never told him how she used to smoke, well before he was born and in truth it wasn't something she had ever intended to let slip. Mary had always done her best raise Paul with a healthy mentality and had given up smoking well before he was born. In truth she had never really been a serious smoker; favoring one here and there when in a social environment where alcohol flowed or, as the present moment had reminded her, after a vigorous roll in the hay. "Oh." She back peddled. "It was never a habit sweetheart. I just used to like one after sex, that's all. But that was many, many years ago." She confessed.

"Maybe you just haven't had the kind of sex to need one in a while." Paul replied with a sheepish grin that reminded Mary of his youth. She jabbed him playfully in the ribs.

"Look who's all cocky now!" She laughed. "But now that you mention it, there might be some truth to that." She sighed as she snuggled up against him again, kicking her legs under her comforter as the air in the room started to bleed off and the chill from the window licked at the moisture on her body.

"Well..." Paul began carefully; too carefully causing Mary to regard him again curiously. "If you really want one..." He added, his face looking like he was preparing for his mother to slap the taste out of his mouth.

"Paul!" Mary gasped. "Do not tell me you smoke!" She sat fully up looking him sternly in the eyes. The ache of all her body's muscles complained at the sudden stern motion. Paul's hands shot up in defense.

"I don't!" He replied. "Well, not really. I just like one if I'm drinking that's all. Phil and I brought some beer up to the ski lodge with us and we picked up a pack of smokes on the ride out of town." He explained, with a look in his eyes that reminded Mary of when he was a young boy trying to get himself out of some wrongdoing that she was telling him off over. Mary relaxed slightly but still wore the countenance of an annoyed mother.

"So you were smoking, and drinking... and you're only 18 so dare I ask where you got the alcohol?" She asked slipping into the assertive mentality that her maternal instincts demanded.

"Phil brought that; I picked up the cigarettes." He admitted looking a little more pleased with himself than he should have. Mary continued to stare at her son for several moments more, until she erupted in hysterical laughter in spite of herself. Paul's cautious expression faded into one of wonder, and through her laughter, Mary felt certain she saw him sigh in relief. "What's so funny?" He asked.

"Nothing." Mary relied, waving the question off as she dabbed tears away from the corners of her eyes. "No it's just that, you remind me of you when I was your age and on top of that I feel like a moron." She said. Paul's curious face indicated she clearly had not explained herself well enough. "Well I mean here I am; here we are... Paul I just crawled off your cock and here I am lecturing you about smoking. My priorities just suddenly felt a little fucked up that's all." She reasoned. Paul smiled in reply, probably more due to the fact that he knew he was out of her crosshairs than the fact that she felt ridiculous.

"So what's the verdict then?" He asked.

"Well if you really want to, you're going to have to do the leg work." Mary replied settling back down against her pillows with a huff. "I'm afraid after what you just put me through, I'm going to be selfish and stay in bed." She grinned. Once again, her son's boyish grin made Mary blush. She watched him rock himself off the bed, his body still moist with perspiration. As he strode out of her bedroom, his cock, still impressively hard, bounced up and down out in front of him. As he stepped from sight, she could not help but bite her lip again as she glared at her son's firm tight rear.

"How the hell is he still hard?!" Mary wondered. She whipped the comforter down and settled deeper into her covers, her body relaxing, sore but satisfied. As she lay there, staring at the wall across from her bed it occurred to her that not once since her son had walked in the front door, relieving her of any maternal panic that he was in a ditch freezing to death, had she felt any pang of guilt. No voice had flooded into her mind, screaming at her to stop the horrible moral crimes she was committing and delighting in. She felt happy; giddy even. Before she could over ponder her new found lease on the situation however, Paul rounded her door frame into the room again, slightly less than hard but still thick and swaying beautifully; his cigarettes in one hand and a make shift ash tray in the other hand comprised of a small white dish from the bowels of the kitchen cupboards that Mary had forgotten was there.

Paul settled down under the blankets next to her and placed the dish on his chest. Then, taking two cigarettes from the pack, he placed both in his mouth and lit them together with an expert flick of a silver Zippo that Mary wondered how long he'd had. He passed one of the cigarettes to her and she set it to her lips, taking a long deep drag from its short golden filter. After a brief sputter in her throat that didn't quite evolve into a coughing fit, the nicotine did its job, sinking into her system with a sensation that felt like being in the company of an old and long forgotten friend. Silently, Mary vowed to work out hard the next day to make up this trivial but uncharacteristic lack of judgment.

"Wow." She sighed as a shallow buzz fizzed in her brain, dulling her senses for a moment. "It's defiantly been a while." She added, tilting the cherry into the dish on Paul's chest to flick away the burnt ash. She watched as Paul drew his own to his mouth, sucking in the smoke like he'd been doing it forever and with a pop of his lips, blew a smoke circle high into the air. "Alright Mr. Professional..." She warned him. "So help me, if I see this become a serious habit with you..."

"What?" He cut her off as he flicked his own ashes into the dish. "No more sex?"

"No that punishes me too." Mary giggled, trying to return her face to a mother's cautionary expression. "But I'll think of something." She half-heartedly threatened.

"I promise." He caved. "You can leave them in your nightstand if you want." He offered, suggesting subliminally that they could both of them, keep the cigarettes in reserve for moments like the one they were in. Mary nodded in approval.

"Well..." She began, her thoughts drifting back to their situation. Paul propped himself up on one elbow to face her.

"Yeah we have to do this sooner or later don't we?" He answered, taking another hit off his cigarette slowly with a look about him that suggested to Mary that he was already assembling his thoughts. She lay beside him silently, allowing him, in fact praying that he would take the lead on their conversation, because she still was at a loss as to how to begin. Too many thoughts had circulated through her mind since the first transgression between them and while she was relieved to feel that she still wasn't being burdened with any negativity about it at the moment, she couldn't really understand that either. "Alright well..." Paul began. "I suppose I've had one question on my mind since this all started happening, so if it's ok I'll start there." He offered. Mary nodded in gratitude. She took another long drag off her cigarette and flicked it against the dish.

"Before I even get into how this all happened, I really want to know this. Are you sorry it did?" He asked sincerely. Mary stared at her son for a moment, allowing the question to absorb. At once a complex series of present and past emotions flooded to the surface of her thoughts. After a moments accounting for them all she finally mashed out her cigarette and returned her attention to her son.

"If you had asked me that question even twenty-four hours ago my answer would have been yes." She finally replied reluctantly. Paul's face remained as fixed as poker players, careful not to reveal any emotion until she had finished. "I've spent the last few days staggering between being so hot for you that I couldn't stop touching myself, to staring into a mirror at someone I didn't feel like I knew, praying to turn back the clock and erase a terrible mistake."

"So you think it was a mistake?" Paul asked. Something about the way he interjected made Mary fairly certain that he hadn't wished to hear that. She wished he had concentrated more on the fact that she had been relentlessly masturbating of late.

"Well I certainly know that I didn't wake up that day and make a conscious decision to have sex with you on purpose Paul. You're my son. I mean, who does that?" She tried to explain, certain that her words were just digging a nice hole for her to crawl into. Paul however didn't react and simply listened. "Anyhow I felt awful. Awful because I'd done it; awful because I couldn't help but want it again." She continued. "But I knew there was something undeniable about you; about us. I didn't really have a grasp on what that was but actually, I think it might finally make sense to me in a way."

"I'm not sure I'm following you." Paul queried, a bit puzzled.

"It came so naturally to us." Mary explained. The words left her mouth like a revelation. "There was nothing forced about it, nothing awkward, I mean beyond the obvious... it was electric. It was incredible and it felt so natural. Feels..." She corrected herself. "It feels so natural. Paul I've never been with a man that sex came this easily with. I don't know whether it's because you're my son and I already love you so much but..." Her voice trailed off as Mary heard herself ramble.

"I think I might have an idea what you mean." Paul consoled her.

"Anyhow, no. I'm not sorry. Not anymore, and I can't begin to tell you what a relief it is to be able to say that because I have been... an absolute train wreck for the last three days Paul." Mary confessed as she reached over her son's body, fumbling her fingers into his pack of cigarettes for a fresh one and lighting it, as if in preparation to ask the most logical counter question. After a long deep inhalation of smoke she found the nerve. "So obviously I have to ask you the same thing."

"Whether I'm sorry that it happened?" Paul asked. "To be honest I've been more confused than sorry." He admitted, drawing out another cigarette for himself and lighting it. "I mean it just never occurred to me." He added, before sucking in a lung full.

"What didn't?" His mother asked.

"You." He answered flatly, waving off his mother's naturally affronted expression. "Having sex with you; having dirty thoughts about you. It never occurred to me." He clarified sincerely. "It's like you said; who does that?" He added, recounting her words. Mary sat silently a moment, wondering for the first time how many people actually might have considered incest. "Before it actually happened, nothing of the kind had ever popped into my head where you were concerned. I mean mom, when you caught me jerking off I was so embarrassed."

"Actually, that's what first did it for me." Mary confessed, feeling her face flush red.

"Really?" Paul asked.

"Oh believe me it was a mixture of emotion." Mary corrected herself. "On one hand I was probably as embarrassed as you but on the other; Paul you have a gorgeous cock. I mean I had no idea!" Mary bubbled as she reached out and placed her hand on her son's manhood, tugging on it gently. "Seeing it, well it made all the other thoughts I was having flood to the surface and before I knew it, fucking you was all I could think about." She admitted as she silently recalled the turmoil of enduring such erotic mental play involving her son. "And though I can't say I ever saw you through the eyes I do now, aside from your cock you are a very attractive young man. Frankly, I feel odd for not seeing it until now." Mary continued to playfully stroke her son as she looked up into his eyes devotedly. Her shoulders felt lighter, free of days of built up fears and self loathing. There was a sense of peace in getting everything out in the open.

"See? Now that makes sense to me." Paul replied through the grin that her hand's affections was causing. I never looked at you like this before all this happened either and now I'm absolutely amazed at how sexy I find you." Mary smiled broadly, unable to help the happiness that such a compliment provided. "So..." Paul sighed with a solemn and intent expression. "The most obvious question is... what now?" Paul asked mashing out his cigarette. Mary did the same with hers.

"I don't want to stop." She confessed. "Paul I don't think I could stop if I did want to." She added, tugging on his cock with a bit more intent. Paul's face dissolved into a moment of bliss before he tried to refocus himself.

"I thought we were talking now." He grinned in pleasure.

"We are. I just can't keep my hands off you." His mother replied, laughing a little but savoring the feel of both of their slippery orgasms smearing between her fingers as she coaxed his cock back to its full state with slow strokes of her hand. "But..." She added suddenly. "I think we need to be a bit more careful."

"I was wondering about that." Paul replied through labored breaths as he tried to concentrate on the conversation despite his mother's efforts. "Are you on birth control?" He asked as his eyes began to flutter closed.

"No, and that's how many times now that you've cum inside me buster?" Mary mused. Paul grinned sheepishly in reply with a shrug of his shoulders to indicate that he too had lost count. "I will go back on the pill but in the meantime..." Mary warned.

"We need protection." Paul replied as he gently took her hand and removed it from his cock. Mary looked back at him with a look of disappointment. "I can't concentrate while you do that." He admitted with a grin.

"I have condoms." She finally said through her protest, pointing towards her nightstand drawer. "I just never can seem to remember them when we need them." Almost immediately, Samantha's suggestion about anal sex came flooding into the forefront of Mary's thoughts, bringing with it a new question. "Paul I actually have a serious question to ask you." She said solemnly.

"No better time than now then." He replied, reminding his mother that the topic of conversation was already a fairly serious one.

"Have you... discussed this with anyone else?" Mary asked with a hint of worry in her tone, not that Paul might have a confidant that he could confess himself to, but rather how he might react to the inevitable confession that she did.

"Are you kidding?!" Paul stammered. "Who could I tell? It's not like I can just pal up to a buddy and be all like, hey man! How are you? I fucked my mother; what are your thoughts?" He added imitating himself jokingly. Mary didn't laugh, but stared at him quietly. "Wait... are you saying you have? Who did you tell?" Paul asked, his tone becoming concerned.

"Paul I need you to understand; at first I was so conflicted about this that I couldn't tell up from down." Mary began, trying to justify her breach in what Paul clearly considered a matter of confidence.

"Who Mom?" He asked again.

"I talked to Samantha and she was very helpful..." Mary began but Paul cut her short.

"Mrs. Conner?!" He blurted out in amazement. "You told Ben's mom?!"

"She is my best friend." Mary defended herself.

"Mom, remember when Mrs. Harris was planning to divorce her husband and because she confided in Mrs. Conner the whole church was talking about it before her husband ever had a clue?" Paul reminded his mother, illustrating in perfect detail the result of Samantha's ability to keep a secret.

"I know; I remember." Mary sighed. "First of all Sam always had a grudge against Susan Harris since way back in the day and you know as well as I do that she's just the type of woman that doesn't let old gripes go so easily. Paul, I've known her most of my life and she's never done something like that to me. I know she's not the best at keeping things to herself but I assure you..." Mary continued but was interrupted again.

"Not the best? She's actually one of the worst." Paul replied, his face welling up in sheer panic.

"Paul, she's thought about Ben." Mary stated simply, ceasing her son's pre-prepared counter arguments. He stared at her confounded. Mary nodded in the affirmative at the question burning through his eyes. "Yes, she's had dirty thoughts about Ben. She hasn't acted on them; come to think of it I kind of doubt she ever would. She seems to be having a fine time living it vicariously though me." Mary laughed as she recalled Samantha's thirst for every tiny detail of her incestuous adventure.

"So she knows..." Paul asked.

"Everything." His mother replied. "In fact, if it weren't for Sam, we probably wouldn't be here right now. Paul I know it freaks you out, and to be honest it does preoccupy me as unwise to have told anyone else too, but I had to talk to someone about what happened between us or I was going to burst. If I could only convey the nightmare of emotions I was dealing with. You left and I had nobody. Well actually it didn't really start there." She realized out loud. "Anyhow she helped calm me down. She told me that the thoughts; the feelings I have for you were alright. She made me feel like I wasn't alone; like I wasn't a horrible freak! I really needed that. I needed to be... ok with it." Mary sighed, understanding for the millionth time how much she owed Samantha as a friend.

"You said it didn't really start there." Paul asked after a moment's consideration.

"I talked to her for the first time about it after I caught you masturbating. Like I said, that's where it all began for me." She replied. "And since then, everything that's happened... well she's kind of coached me through it. Paul I promise you, she won't say a word to anyone." She related, hoping that the trust she expressed for Sam would carry over to her son's confidence. He didn't seem convinced.

"Well, you're a hell of a lot luckier than I am." Paul answered after absorbing everything he had learned. "I was up in the mountains with Phil. God knows I wanted to talk to someone about it, but I don't think Phil would have been my first choice."

"It's a girl thing." Mary chuckled, offering some consolation to her son's obviously less fortunate predicament. "With us it comes easier to talk about things." Mary explained warmly, deciding silently not to allude to the second half of the Samantha equation just yet.

"Better to introduce that at another time." She told herself, but at that moment, her arousal spiked somewhere deep inside her at the prospect of applying Samantha's suggestion and instruction about alternate sex with Paul. Mary brushed the thought aside; they were still talking and she had more to ask. To say nothing of the fact that if Paul now felt half as connected to her as she did to him, revealing what she and Sam had done might have been viewed as some sort of twisted infidelity. As she considered it like that, Mary almost felt guilty but resigned herself to staying silent on the matter so as to stay on track.

"Women have secrets for a reason." She thought to herself.

"Are you alright?" She asked, seeing if she could bring the topic to a close in favor of a new one.

"Yeah I guess. I was just, surprised that's all." Paul admitted. "I wouldn't think you'd dare talk about this with anyone."

"And I have no intention of talking about it with anyone else." Mary reassured her son. "But I do have one other question for you. It's probably the least important one out of the lot but I do really want to know."

"Shoot." Paul replied. Mary leaned in close and pressed her lips passionately against her son's, opening his mouth with her lips and moaning softly as her tongue tasted his before breaking away again.

"Where did you learn to make love like you do?!" She growled playfully offering her son's cock another pleasurable tug. Paul burst into laughter causing her to join him. He reached his arm out wrapped her up in it. Mary sighed in comfort against his body and continued to happily play with his penis, which twitched delightfully at her soft touches.

"Well...um..." Paul began; his cheeks crimson with a boyish embarrassment.

"Oh come on!" Mary exclaimed. "I hardly think you need to go all shy on me now." She added as she drew her hand up to her lips and adoringly licked a trickle of Paul's pre-ejaculate from her fingertips as though completely unable to help herself. "Ok I'll make this easier. How many girls have you been with?" She asked, returning her hand to his stiffening erection to gingerly stroke it up and down. He moaned and it swelled in her grip.

"Only two." He replied through ragged breaths. Mary's eyes widened in amazement.

"Just two?" She replied, stroking his cock faster in her hands. Paul grumbled hoarsely in pleasure.

"The first was a girl I never actually told you about." Paul admitted. "Remember that school lock-in my junior year?" He continued. Mary nodded and then propped her head up in curiosity.

"Wait... you're telling me you lost your virginity in your high school?!" She asked, truly stunned. "Wasn't that lock-in chaperoned?"

"Well yeah, but she and got to talking, and then we were making out and one thing led to another and..." He mumbled as Mary released his cock and began to gently run her fingernails across his testicles.

"Well obviously you snuck away from the group." She remarked, coaxing him to continue.

"We snuck into my history class and did it on the teacher's desk." Paul laughed. Mary stared up at him in amazement.

"And the second girl?" She enquired, wanting to hear more.

"That was Erin." Paul replied, shutting his eyes as he surrendered more to his mother's skillful fingers.

"Your ex? Well that makes more sense I guess. You two were together for a while." Mary reasoned out loud. She remembered Erin well. A slender girl of extremely Greek decent with pretty features and silky dark hair that Mary had once been very jealous of. Her manners were always exceptional. Mary had always liked Erin and been sad for her son when things between them had gone south. "Well... you two must have had some serious practice because you my darling son are an incredible lover!" She complimented, tilting her head down to kiss Paul's chest warmly.

"Not as much as you might think, and it was nothing like this." Paul replied, sending a hot wave of self esteem through Mary that made her blush.

"Nothing like this?" She repeated the statement. Mary was suddenly alight with personal pride to hopefully be ranked supreme in her son's conquests, such as they were.

"Erin was great, but the sex was..." Paul stopped short with a look that suggested to Mary that he was trying to be polite.

"Tame?" Mary offered.

"I almost said boring actually." Paul laughed but stopped himself, drawing back to the same polite reserve. Mary smiled at her son proudly, respecting the fact that even after a break up, he was more inclined to speak well of a person. "I was her first and even after things become easier between us, she was really reserved." Paul tried to explain. "I wanted to try to be more experimental; more intense. Erin on the other hand always seemed scared." He reflected, obviously hoping that the vagueness in his words would suffice his mother's curiosity. "So anyhow, there hasn't been anyone since her until you and the difference is indescribable." Paul lastly offered, hoping to shift the subject back in a direction he felt like discussing.

"Well I know you like older women." Mary said, returning her hand to Paul's throbbing cock and continuing to coax his rich young pre-cum from the head.

"Huh?" Paul asked, taken aback slightly.

"I watched the movie I caught you jerking off to." Mary admitted, leaving out the precise details of that event deliberately so as not to return to Samantha. Paul's face went red again, causing Mary to giggle. "It's nothing to be embarrassed about. Actually it kind of helps me to know you are attracted to women my age." She offered, brining the color in his cheeks down a notch.

"Yes..." Paul whispered. "I do like older women more."

"Well I'm sure I feel nothing like Erin did." Mary offered, fishing for the inevitable compliment with all the false coyness she could convey. Paul laughed.

"You're right. Nothing at all; so much better." He answered properly. Mary groaned in spite of herself; her self confidence brimming over and carrying her arousal along for the ride.

"Is my pussy nice and tight like hers?" Mary giggled, seeing how much she could get away with.

"Keep talking like that and we'll go again just to make sure." Paul replied with a deep growl in his voice. His mother's eyes widened in what she was certain would be easily confused with terror. "Or not..." Paul laughed, summing up her concern. "We don't have to if..." He began.

"If what?" Mary whispered, hesitantly snuggling closer to him.

"If... you feel you can't..." Paul cautiously began.

"Take it?" Mary sharply finished, looking at her son incredulously. Paul smiled sheepishly, realizing that he had just implied that he had broken her. Despite her own concern, the idea made Mary desperate to prove the idea utter nonsense. "Don't go making me feel like some old woman now!" She added with a playfully stern look. Without another word Paul leaned over her and slid her legs apart with his until he was resting above her supported on his arms.

"God he's insatiable!" She thought as she permitted herself to be mounted.

Mary stared down her body, mesmerized but fearful of the size of her son's bounding erection after all that her body had already endured that night. He knelt between her legs, holding the instrument of her reservation in his hand. Mary's pulse quickened at the majesty of her son's form. She watched as he set the head of his cock upon her clit and rubbed across it slowly. Her eyes fluttered in their sockets as the phallic massage lowered; the head of his cock drawing slowly up and down between her vaginal lips. His demeanor was one of caution and care as he teased her mercilessly until she felt the warm seep of her juices reply through her core to her stretched and wanton opening. Biting her lip, Mary braced her body for the glorious inevitable. Inhaling sharply, Mary surrendered to her son's tireless libido as he pressed his girth slowly back into her flooding channel.

"Oh God, Paul go slowly. I'm still so sensitive." Mary moaned, tilting her head back into her pillow with her eyes closed; feeling her son slide gently in and out of her tormented vagina. Paul leaned in, taking advantage of her exposed throat, washing his lips in delicate kissed along the side of her neck. His hands cradled her up, holding himself tightly to her as he moved just his hips, sinking his manhood between her swollen labia in deep lethargic strokes.

"I love you so much." Paul's voice whispered in his mother's ear. It sounded like the words of a lover, blended with the perfect devotion a child bestowed upon a parent. Mary lifted her legs, tangling them tightly around her son's hips and tugging his body into hers with each stroke of his penis into her.

"Oh baby I love you too." Mary gasped, feeling her heart flutter down into the pit of her stomach and offering supporting argument to Samantha's accusation from earlier that day. She rolled her head back down, staring up into his eyes. They burned into somewhere deep inside of Mary. She felt open to him; completely without reservation. She gazed back, softly whimpering in pleasure as he made love to her. He was reading her to her core, attentive to her every signal. Mary couldn't believe how attuned he was to her and wondered if perhaps it was the familiarity that only a mother and son could share. She was safest with him. As this realization set in, it reminded her of the trust she had shown Sam earlier and without warning, her anus began to tingle. Mary swallowed hard.

"I'd like to try something." She whispered. The simplicity of her words brought her son's hips still and calm. He gazed down at her curiously. Mary felt her face flush warmly, but the mental image of her son taking her where no man had ever successfully been battled through her shyness. She reached down and gently pressed his hips back until his cock painfully withdrew from her. Not saying another word for fear of a request psyching her out, she rolled over onto her belly.

"Like this..." She whispered, staring at her headboard for fear of making eye contact. Behind her, she felt Paul press his cock head back against her pussy reservedly. "No baby..." She whispered, pulling away. Sighing heavily, she looked back and grasped Paul's cock in her hand, pulling him forward and guiding the bulging head slowly and fearfully towards her tingling ass. "Like this..." She repeated. Slowly, she looked back to meet his eyes which possessed an almost tangible amazement.

"I've never..." He began. Mary shook her head.

"Me either." She half lied. "I want the first time to be with you." She added, gulping down the pounding in her heart. Paul, perhaps sensing her terror leaned in placing his lips delicately on hers. His kiss was more than sensual, it was compassionate. It promised safety.

"You'll have to tell me how." Paul admitted in a barely audible whisper. Mary smiled nervously.

"Go slow." She instructed and turned her head back and rested it on her pillow. The pressure of her son's cock against her tightest and most guarded area felt enormous as Mary did all she could not to wince and scare him off. The pressure built, pushing against her and breaking her slowly open. Mary clenched her teeth into her pillow and tried not to make a sound until she was sure one way or the other. The head pushed completely in forcing a gasp from her lungs. It felt so much larger than fingers. At once the sting she had expected spread through her bowels. Panic gripped at her senses as she bit into the pillow so hard her jaw ached. She knew she was clenching around Paul though she felt powerless to help it.

"Are you alight?" Paul nervously asked, pausing in that moment of finally forcing her open. Mary nodded still not trying to betray her wishes to her fears. Again and again, the mental imagery of her son taking her ass and of her delighting in it gave her strength to continue.

"Just... hold there a moment. Let me get used to it." She finally managed to say as she relaxed her teeth, hoping that the rest of her body would follow suit and relax as well. Paul remained motionless. "How does that feel?" She asked after a moment.

"So tight..." Was all her son could meagerly reply. It wasn't the exact description Mary had hoped for but she couldn't fault him for it. The burn of her stretched opening had begun to subside at last, prompting further bravery.

"Ok, a little more now." She offered. Paul began to thrust, short pulses of motion that slowly crept his cock inch by inch into her ass in slippery strokes that were well lubricated from her still achingly wet vagina. The foreign sensation was such a mixture of feeling. On one hand, Mary could not help but feel invaded, but despite the strangeness of the encounter there was something indescribably intimate about it. Bit by bit she felt her rectum expand, accommodating her son's ample girth. As his cock slid along the thin tissue separating the channels of her two aching holes however, Mary felt the tiny hairs on the back of her neck stand erect as her skin flushed with goose bumps.

"Oh wow..." She mumbled beginning to realize the same intense pleasure Sam had delivered her. "Just like that Paul. Slow...smooth... it feels wonderful!" She whimpered. "God, how far in are you?" She asked.

"About half way. Oh God Mom!" Paul groaned in pleasure. Mary's eyes widened in renewed terror.

"Half way? That's it? You're kidding me?" She gasped as she looked over her shoulder at Paul's pleasured but wary expression. As if to prove it to her, her son leaned in, driving a few more inches of his shaft inside her. "Holy Shit!" Mary exclaimed in disbelief. Involuntarily she felt the walls of her rectum contract around the intrusion.

"God that feels good!" Paul panted, rocking his slippery cock in and out of her ass in long fluid thrusts. "Do that again." He begged. Realizing what he was talking about, Mary willfully squeezed at his cock with her inner muscles. The feeling brought them both to moaning heavily.

"Like that baby?" She whispered. "You like when I squeeze it like that?" She added with another tight clench

"God yes!" Paul exclaimed, finally at last settling his legs tightly alongside his mother's thighs as he pressed the last of his cock inside her until he had no more to offer her gaping ass.

"Oh my God! Oh my fucking God!" Mary groaned.

"He's fucking my ass! He's really doing it!" She marveled silently delighted at the success.

"You can't imagine how sexy this looks." Paul grunted. Mary felt almost certain she could feel his eyes on the stretched flesh of her anus gripping at his cock. She wished she could see it too.

"Oh baby. Do I look good with your cock in my ass?" She asked boldly. "Do you like me like this? Taking you like this?" She added between heavy labored breaths. "Oh my God Paul it feels so good!" Mary wailed as Paul began to take her harder. She felt his hands grasp her cheeks, pushing them apart as he reared back and sank in harder and deeper with each thrust. Mary's head began to swim in its own delicious erotic images of how breathtaking the pair of them had to look locked in so many taboos at once. Paul answered with his body, driving himself into her with vigorous intent. "Don't stop!" Mary cried out each time his pace faltered for fear that he was concerned for her. She was beyond any pain or fear. She had returned to the plane where her world was her son's massive cock; drunk and delirious on what he was capable of doing to her with it.

"Mom!" Paul panted repeatedly between breaths.

"Fuck my ass Paul!" Mary groaned. "Don't stop till you cum. I want to feel that. God baby I never knew..." She mumbled. "I never ever knew it could be like this! Don't you stop Paul. Don't stop till you fill me!"

The room around her had dissolved into blackness. Whether that was because of the intensity or the fact that Mary had to nearly keep her eyes closed to fight off tears of pleasure, she could no longer be certain. Her nostrils drank in the thick mist of their lovemaking hovering in the air. Every fiber of what made up her body tingled and danced under her skin. Above her, Paul shifted his weight, spearing his cock in an entirely different angle that made her vagina spasm. Before she could announce it, Mary felt her core gush. Bearing down, she felt it erupt from her swollen labia like a fountain, squirting unbearably hard against her mattress as Paul relentlessly hammered into her ass. Barely a sound escaped her lips as she lay flat and climaxed endlessly until spent. The saturation from her vagina splashed against her son's heavily swinging testicles and offered lewd slapping sounds between them as he brought his weight into each pelvic motion.

"Oh God that looks so good!" Paul groaned. Before Mary could register what he meant she felt him pull back; his cock popping from her sucking anus before digging its way back into the flooded depths of her pussy.

"Paul! Fuck!" She screamed as he pounded effortlessly towards her womb as hard as she felt certain he was capable of. "God fuck me!" She babbled as the tears she had fought to restrain flooded from her eyes. Behind her, her son grunted as he filled her over and over again. Her abused channel was raw and stinging. Her rear felt spanked raw as the torrent of slaps from his hips beat against it. "Paul I'm yours. Do whatever you want! Take me! I'm yours!" She cried out again, unable to move or think; certainly unable to provide any protest had she found reason to offer it. His thighs felt ironclad as the held her hips in place. Rolling her head over to the other side, her eyes met the glow of her bedside alarm clock. It shimmered a time six hours past when Paul had first arrived home. Looking up towards her window, through the slits of her blinds the sun was creeping over the horizon. Mary shuttered with disbelief.

"God I want your ass again." Paul groaned, breaking Mary's attention back to the moment. As she babbled incoherently in affirmation, her son speared back into her rectum, filling it completely in a single harsh push. "Mom! Oh yes!" He panted as he fucked her. "Tell me to cum!" He begged. Mary could already feel him swell inside her. She knew there wasn't a choice.

"Fill me lover. Fill my ass. Give me your cum!" She shouted as she spread her legs along her mattress, trying desperately to offer her son's cock the deepest penetration. As she did, the walls of her womb trembled. "Oh God Paul I'm going to cum. Cum with me. Fill me. Fuck me! I'm cumming!" Mary screamed as her son's exasperated wail behind her heralded the orgasm that pulsed into her rectum in hot sloppy squirts. "Oh Paul yes!" She cried as the intensity crested, drowning out everything. Her heartbeat gonged in her ears and her muscled contracted as her body rode the waves of their pleasure filing her and escaping her. With a heavy slump of fatigue, Paul collapsed against her back. He was sweaty and hot and wrapped his limbs around her like a protective blanket. Still lodged deeply inside her, he rolled to the side, taking her with him in his tight embrace. Neither had will or capability to speak for an endless span of minutes that were spent catching breath and relaxing the fiery impulses in their loins. Mary had never known such contentment.

"How does this feel so right?" Paul whispered after some time. The question was rhetorical but it brought back into sharp relief a curiosity in Mary that she had been dreading returning to.

"Paul I want to say something to you and I'm not sure how." Mary whispered.

"Just say it to me Mom." Paul replied, keeping her held very closely against him. "I think we're past pulling punches." His reply was calm but cold and Mary felt certain he was bracing himself for some inevitable let-down. She collected her thoughts meticulously before continuing.

"I still don't know what this is; it's incredible but I don't want it to change your life." Mary began, realizing that her words weren't quite conveying the intent she wished to express. "What I mean is I can't imagine a world now where this ends, but some day you'll meet someone..." She continued before Paul cut her off.

"Mom..." He began, trying to be reassuring.

"Paul, let me finish. I don't want to stop you from having a normal life; normal relationships. Some day you will in fact meet someone; someone who you want to be with. Someone that you want to spend your life with. That can never be me; not outside closed doors anyway. I want you to know I expect that to happen. When it does, I want to know." Mary said. The words caught in her throat like a painful reality but she swallowed it down. "And I want to know so that we can end this the right way." She added. "I haven't the first clue what the right way is yet, but we can figure that out along the way. I want you to be able to date and be a young man. You aren't restricted to me ok?" Mary asked.

"Then you aren't either." Paul replied. "If you're going to tell me that I'm not exclusive to you then I shouldn't expect anything different."

"Oh please Paul I'm 40 years old and..." Mary began.

"And incredibly hot and have a lot to offer anyone." Paul replied, cutting her short with the reassuring and heartfelt compliment. Mary smiled broadly, even though she knew her son couldn't see it as he held her back against his chest.

"Right now the only one I'm offering anything to is you. I'm yours." She replied. "Paul some part of me is battling with the idea that I might be in love with you, and for the first time in days I'm at peace with that." Mary whispered. "I don't want things to change but someday they will."

"Someday isn't today." Paul replied. "It's not likely to be tomorrow either. What I'm saying is let someday be someday. Let right now be right now."

Mary arched her back, settling deeper into her son's arms and shut her eyes, drowning out the dawn's rays that were banding her room through her blinds in narrow bright slits. They felt heavy and demanded rest. She knew that someday was closer than she wanted, but resigned to her son's logic for total lack to fight it.

"Someday..." She whispered.

"But not today..." He said again, leaning in to kiss the back of her neck lovingly.

"I love you so much Paul." Mary's voice trailed off as she allowed sleep to take her, returning to the satisfaction that her son was holding her, that he was still inside her where she knew he belonged.

"I love you too Mom."

THE END

Share your thoughts with us.
Take a moment to tell us how we're doing. Your feedback really matters.

You can reach us by:
Email: my777books@yahoo.com

Search for other titles by **Sophie MacDonald.**

www.ingramcontent.com/pod-product-compliance
Lightning Source LLC
LaVergne TN
LVHW011253200326
834410LV00006B/237